THE **KAYLA** Chronicles

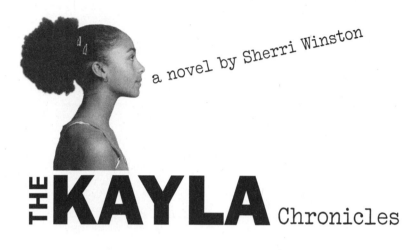

a novel by Sherri Winston

THE **KAYLA** Chronicles

LITTLE, BROWN AND COMPANY
New York ❧ Boston

To my beautiful daughters, Lauren and Kenya.
Mommy loves you!

Little, Brown and Company

Hachette Book Group USA
237 Park Avenue, New York, NY 10017
Visit our Web site at www.lb-teens.com

First Edition: September 2007

ISBN-13: 978-0-316-11430-1
ISBN-10: 0-316-11430-8

10 9 8 7 6 5 4 3 2 1

Book design by Alison Impey

Q-MT

Printed in the United States of America

ACKNOWLEDGMENTS

I would like to thank everyone who helped me take *The Kayla Chronicles* from dream to reality.

Jennifer Hunt, thanks for believing in me and being the finest editor I've ever worked with. And to my agent, George Nicholson, and his assistant, Thaddeus Bower, thank you guys for hanging in there with me.

Also, a special thanks to "The Friday Group." Without the love and support of Joyce, Norma, Dorian, Gloria, Alex, and all the other great writers in our group, Kayla might still be an idea rather than a reality.

And finally, my deepest gratitude to my sisters and brothers. Thanks for the babysitting, the shoulders to cry on, the endless supply of confidence when mine was lacking. And thanks to my daughters, Kenya and Lauren, for helping me coin the phrase "stankalicious." Mommy loves you!

SHY GIRL SPARKS A REVOLUTION!

Stankalicious!

Allow me to define it:

Stank-a-le-shus — derived from *stank,* slang for *stinker;* 1) the art of being stank; 2) one who behaves in a manner so over-board, so bigger-than-life outrageous, so self-deluded, well, it could only be considered *stankalicious.*

And *stankalicious,* the newest word in my book of *Kayla-isms,* describes my best friend, Rosalie, to a tee.

You won't believe what she wants me to do. And all in the name of feminism. *Hmph!*

NEWS FLASH: Feminism did not start at the home of Rosalie Renée Hunter and a feminist is not automatically a fashion-hating, man-hating, cause-spouting rebel-rouser.

When I, Mikayla Alicia Dean, soon to be fifteen, think of feminism, I think of strong females taking action — even when that action goes against the girly-girl mold society assigns us.

Think Xena: Warrior Princess. Amelia Earhart. Venus and Serena Williams. Buffy the Vampire Slayer. And my late Grandma JoJo. Not just strong, but distinctive, too.

And then there's Nellie Bly, the butt-kicking, role-reversing turn-of-the-century journalist who practically invented investigative journalism. I can't wait for my chance to be like her. To go undercover and find the real-deal lowdown on who's doing dirt and who's getting hurt, you know?

Here's what feminism is not:

* ✳ **Girls who back down**
* ✳ **Girls seeking "prince charming"**
* ✳ **Young women obsessed with marriage**

Oooo! When I see a girl acting all Pepto-princessy (sweet, super icky, ultra girly, guaranteed to make you sick to your stomach), I'm right there with Rosalie. I think we women need to stand together and ditch that pseudo-feminine crutch. Know what I mean?

My goal in life is to spark a quiet, purposeful revolution. I see myself as a tastefully dressed, soft-spoken, determined young woman.

Wearing really cool shoes.

Meanwhile, Rosalie wants to serve as supreme ruler of an

all-female encampment where men are forced to plow fields and walk dogs and must not speak unless told to.

And cute shoes would be punishable by *Rosilaw*!

Today Rosalie unleashed her most stupendous *stankalicious* scheme yet. Totally twisted and certain to doom my future.

First, she announced that SPEAK—Sisters Providing Encouragement And Kindness—the club I started in middle school, has been officially sanctioned as a club/activity at our new high school thanks to her nonstop lobbying.

That's bad enough, but it's not the "doom my future" part. The "doom my future" part is that she wants me to try out for the Lady Lions dance team—the *It* girls of our new school. She wants me to prove how they won't let ordinary girls like me on the team. So my goal is to fail, thus supporting her theory while turning me into a huge "Who Not To Be Like" poster.

Rosalie was all "ooo" and "ahhh" and "power to the people," and I'm like, "hmm, you have a lot of nerve, sister-girl. A. Lot. Of. Nerve."

I didn't say it out loud, though.

I should have, but I didn't.

See, this was the problem. If I were a superheroine, my cape would have the letters *SP* stitched across the back for "Super Pathetic." Unfortunately, my superhuman power is the ability to hold back my true thoughts and feelings.

But I swear that's going to end.

Way back, Rosalie's mom, Dr. X, told both of us we should keep a list of declarations, a short list of what we will and will not do to remind us of who we are and what we stand for. My list.

I WILL:

✳ Be more assertive and stand up for what is right for me.

✳ Leave behind the shy old me and embrace the brand-new bold me.

✳ Be firm but fair and loving when faced with adversity.

✳ Fight to be the kind of journalist I've always wanted to be; one who takes risks, one who isn't afraid, one who makes a difference.

✳ Honor the memory of my Grandma JoJo by embracing all the values and strengths that she held dear — being a strong black woman and an intellectual. [That one just added.]

I WILL NOT:

✳ Get distracted by frivolity.

✳ Compromise my values just to please someone else.

✳ Give up on myself.

✳ Allow myself to be bullied.

✳ Be afraid.

And I intend to follow my list, too. If I can just get over what happened at Rosalie's tonight.

HURRICANE WATCH:
Will emotional storm blow Kayla off course?

It is easier to live through someone else than to become complete yourself. — Betty Friedan

Believe it or not, my A-cup breasts are pawns in a vicious power struggle.

At least, they would be if Rosalie gets her way.

Last night, Rosalie revealed her secret plan. Today she is trying to set it in motion. I, on the other hand, would like to set myself on fire. I wonder if Joan of Arc started out this way.

Rosalie's plan goes like this:

She wants me to try out for one of Florida's most renowned dance teams, Royal Palm Academy's Lady Lions, but undercover, like an investigative reporter, and expose their practice of choosing only girls with big, luscious breasts.

You know, unlike mine, which are small. Microscopic.

I wanted to cry, except crying would have played right into the popular myth of inherent female weakness.

"They can't get away with discriminating against girls with small breasts. No way. SPEAK won't stand for it," Rosalie said. We were in my bedroom. My head was pounding. Rosalie was pacing; I was sitting cross-legged in the middle of my bed. Biting my nails.

And practically choking on what I wanted to say but what I knew I wouldn't say.

She said, "SPEAK is going to crash through the present, male-driven power structure at Royal and make strong women, women with a brain, respected!"

Translation: She was on a mission—a mission to humiliate me in front of the entire school, maybe even the world.

See, SPEAK was a small club I started in middle school. Mainly, it was a safe haven for those of us who didn't want to sit like lepers, shoved to the corners of the cafeteria. With some help from my grandmother and a few other parents, we became a close-knit group that discussed books, shopped together, had sleepovers, and did community service projects together.

Then Rosalie moved to our school and soon we went from a little club to vigilantes for women's rights. I started SPEAK, but now Rosalie had gotten us an actual club charter at our new high school, Royal Palm Academy. Yes, "the big league."

So now, she had a plan that would make SPEAK come out fighting. It would work like this:

Prove dance-team tryouts were stacked in favor of, well, "the stacked."

How? By using my eleven years of gymnastics training and secret love of dancing to try out, then get humiliated with a resounding, "Take a hike, you flat-chested girl-boy."

Then, because I was majoring in journalism, I was supposed to write an exposé and reveal discrimination against girls Rosalie proudly referred to as members of the "itty-bitty club."

The whole scene replayed in my head like a bad hygiene film from fifth grade, but I didn't completely shoot her down. Here's why.

Ambition. Crazy, blind ambition. Sometimes, I close my eyes and I see myself shiny-faced with the glow of justice, pen and paper in hand, with a legion of equally bosom-challenged girls alongside me, chanting my name. And I see the headlines:

Kayla Dean Infiltrates Dance Team
Senate Probes Plight of Itty-Bitties
A-cups Get Their Due!

Well, a girl can dream, can't she?

Rosalie frantically plowed through my closet, pulling out one shirt or skirt after another. T-shirts with "Save the Manatees" or "Greenpeace" logos floated to the floor. I sat with my feet tucked under my butt, my hands drumming a beat on my thighs.

She was searching for a uniform for my humiliation. Why couldn't she leave it alone? Wasn't she as tired of being an outcast as I was?

Going to RPA is a big deal.

And its journalism program—**HUGE!**

"Who cares about Royal Palm's top-ranking journalism program or award-winning women's studies program," she blared, as though reading my thoughts, "when the reigning symbol of school pride is those butt-shaking, midriff-baring go-go dancers from the suburbs? Think about their big fundraisers. Washing cars in cut-offs and bikini tops. It's an insult to women everywhere! Those girls make that dance squad for one reason. Because of their big . . . big . . ."

Her hands pulsed outward. In and out, in and out.

"Breasts!" Rosalie snarled. "They all have really big breasts. No itty-bitties like you and me." After that last part she actually sagged against my closet door. Her fury spent.

Please remember: The Lady Lions are a dance team. Not militants or bank robbers. I swear, she was blowing so much hot air I was scared she might crack the windows—between all her wind and the howling tropical rainstorm outside the barometric pressure could drop and suck us through the glass. Maybe that wouldn't be such a bad thing.

"Rozy, I . . ." My mouth was dry. My heart was beating fast. I would've given anything to be back in the old house where me and JoJo, my grandmother, lived back when the rest of the family was overseas. That was before JoJo died and Mom came back from her photography gig in Africa, bringing my Army dad and stuck-up baby sister with her.

"Um, Rozy, I mean, Rosalie, uh, um, this won't, I mean, work." My face was burning. I was such a loser. Why was this so hard? I was close to passing out just thinking about it.

Like the mighty cheetah, fast and furious, she pounced.

"Before you say you can't, let me remind you why you MUST do this!"

Even the lizard clinging to the wood railing above my bathroom froze, horrified to hear Rosalie's *list* yet again. Rosalie's reasons for hating the Lady Lions, as I and the lizard well knew, went as follows:

1. Last fall's school newspaper, *The Clarion*. School board member quote: "The Lady Lions embody the best of what young womanhood is all about."

2. Rumors that when the dance team made it to the nationals, the principal redirected money meant for the girls' softball team and the debate team to pay Lady Lions' expenses.

3. Her cousin, Giselle, didn't make the dance team last year and she convinced Rosalie it was her cup size that killed her.

"It is time to knock the Lady Lions off their pedestal, and SPEAK will have an immediate presence, *chica*, wait and see."

I wanted to jump off my bed and tell her how much I didn't care about the plan. Tell her how secretly I'd always thought about trying out and now, thanks to her, I was going to do it, only I wasn't doing it just as part of some sinister, girl-power plot.

Wanted to—but didn't.

Pathetic, party of one, right this way, please.

She looked at me, and her expression made me groan.

"Okay, who said this? 'We live in a world which respects power above all things'?"

"Rozy, not the quotes."

Several years ago, JoJo required her college students to memorize quotes one semester, and Rosalie and I did it, too. JoJo got us hooked on an Internet site with quotes from famous women.

That used to seem so cool to me; now it just made me feel like some über geek. I had moved on, or at least I had tried. But Rosalie pushed ahead.

If I told her, would she even care?

She returned her attention to my closet, calling over her shoulder, "Mary McLeod Bethune, that's who said it. The founder of Bethune-Cookman College up in Daytona, remember now?" Then she went back to digging through my stuff and dissing my clothes.

A Billie Holiday quote came to mind:

Sometimes it's worse to win a fight than to lose.

"Perfect!" Rosalie spun around, holding a black unitard with a red stripe slashed diagonally across the midsection. Mom bought it for me. I'd never worn it, though. Clung too much to my big b-o-o-t-y.

Just so you know, I have a lot of booty.

Rosalie tossed it and commanded, "Try it on!" When I came out of the bathroom wearing the hideous and too revealing unitard, my cutesy younger sister, Amira, stuck her head inside the bedroom. She looked from me to Rosalie and frowned.

"I see you're having another Sisters Who Need Makeovers meeting."

That Amira, only thirteen but already the funniest girl she knew. So perky and perfect. *Ugh!* Unlike me, with my ultra flatness on top and freakish roundness on bottom. "Mom wants to see you."

"Why?" I asked.

She shrugged. My stomach knotted. Mom and I were like spies with the same agency but working on vastly different save-the-world scenarios. Lately, she'd been acting all let-me-be-your-best-friend and I was just not feeling her. Grandma JoJo practically raised me. She was my best friend. Sometimes . . . well, me and my mother were not that close. I wanted her to leave me alone.

But at the same time, I really didn't want her to leave me alone. So I didn't know what I wanted from her—or my father. No way to explain it.

"K, you are it, girl," Rosalie went on, ignoring Amira, who smirked and slammed the door. "No one can deny you're a true member of the itty-bitty society!" She raised both arms upwards in a *V* like refs do when there's a touchdown.

Kayla is flat-chested. Score!

Rosalie grabbed me by the shoulders. "I told Dr. X all about the plan. She thinks it's brilliant." Rosalie leaned closer. In a half whisper, she said, "Dr. X thinks Miss JoJo would see this as the perfect way to honor her memory on your upcoming happy fifteenth."

My face felt hot. She had no right acting like she or her

mother could know what was in my grandmother's heart. JoJo died almost a year ago. She merely tolerated Dr. X, calling her sanctimonious and self-righteous! How JoJo and I had planned to celebrate my turning fifteen was private and personal. I was biting the inside of my lip so hard I thought it might bleed!

"Chica!" Rosalie snapped her fingers. Secretly, I referred to her as "the Convenient Latina." Not since JLo, the early years, have I witnessed someone slip in and out of ethnicity with such ease.

"Kayla!" she barked. All-American, once again. I blinked.

"So you'll do it, right, Kayla? You'll do it, no more hesitation?" She moved in for the kill. "Do it and you'll have the best inside high school journalism story of the year. JoJo told you she figured out her calling to be a professor when she turned fifteen. Now it's your turn. Your calling is investigative reporting. And it's calling you right now."

I couldn't talk, so I just nodded. Rosalie reached out and pulled me into a huge hug. She was shorter than me, and in the mirror I felt like our insides had become as mismatched as our outsides.

So it was official:

My boy-breasts were about to become political prisoners in a high-stakes game of Popularity Death Match.

Breasts so small shouldn't be so much trouble.

TO: dragonslayer@webtv.net
FROM: ladygodiva@bellnet.net

How did you know about the letter?

TO: ladygodiva@bellnet.net
FROM: dragonslayer@webtv.net

My cousin, Giselle, she's in that program, too.

TO: dragonslayer@webtv.net
FROM: ladygodiva@bellnet.net

Well, as if I don't have enough to deal with, journalism depart-ment's letter is reminding us to pay attention to local headlines and news and "stay aware" before our big orientation session later in the month.

TO: ladygodiva@bellnet.net
FROM: dragonslayer@webtv.net

"Self-development is a higher duty than self-sacrifice." Elizabeth Cady Stanton.

TO: dragonslayer@webtv.net
FROM: ladygodiva@bellnet.net

Oh, no, not the quotes again. My whole body hurts from doing dance routine over and over; still not sure about this. Don't think I'm ready for this.

TO: ladygodiva@bellnet.net
FROM: dragonslayer@webtv.net

U can do this, K. You've been dancing forever. U R an amazing gymnast. U R good enough to be on that dance team.

TO: dragonslayer@webtv.net
FROM: ladygodiva@bellnet.net

"I want a busy life, a just mind, and a timely death." — Zora Neale Hurston. I'm all for the cause, but right now, U R killing me.

TO: ladygodiva@bellnet.net
FROM: dragonslayer@webtv.net

"Where there is no struggle, there is no strength." — Oprah Winfrey. U will vindicate others, like my cousin, Giselle, cut unfairly because of their measurements instead of their talents. G'night. See you day after tomorrow. Meet at your house before tryouts.

FAMILY PORTRAIT

How does the family outcast fit in the picture?

For what do we live, but to make sport for our neighbors, and laugh at them in our turn? — Jane Austen

Our backyard barbecue was a dramatic scene straight out of a Jane Austen novel turned on its head. What started out as the perfect opportunity to mock the relatives and observe bizarre male-female rituals among adult humans soon turned into a twisted, psycho-cultural soap opera that left me questioning my utter disregard for the institution of marriage and missing my grandmother more than I had since her funeral.

The events were as follows:

Mom caught up with me. I'd managed to sidestep her since the other day, but she finally got me. Wanted to tell me she was thinking about a part-time job with Metro-Zoo in Miami, doing a photo chronicle of the animals.

"But I wanted to talk to you about it first. Maybe you and I . . ."

She looked like she was going to suggest we needed to spend "quality time" together. I couldn't handle "quality time." Really.

"Please, you should do it," I'd said. Then I ran, almost getting away, but instead ran right into Amira and two of our cousins who were in the den watching music videos.

"Kayla, wanna watch videos with us?" one of the girls asked.

"She doesn't watch television," Amira chimed before I could answer. It was true. I tried not to watch much broadcast television. The commercials. The ads are designed to make people, especially women, feel inferior.

"No, thanks," I said.

"Why won't she watch TV? Is she Amish?" asked the other cousin. I could never remember their names.

Amira shook her head. "Nope. Just boring."

Later, while I sat in a lotus position channeling my yoga calm, Daddy Dearest stunned, stunned, STUNNED us all.

Okay, here's some info that won't shock you, I'm sure:

My father and I, we just don't see eye-to-eye. Since retiring from the army, he's been running his own construction firm. Very alpha male. When I tell him he's "totally male," he thinks it's a compliment.

It is *sooo* not.

I call him either "Father" or "the Great Oppressor." Amira calls him "Daddy-daddy." Like she's stuttering . . . or worse, in awe. The entire time he, my mom, and Amira were traveling, they'd come back here for extended periods of time. I don't know why, but I just never felt comfortable around him. He's nice enough, as males go, but after living with JoJo and it being just us, having a man around was sorta like entertaining a visitor from another planet. I just didn't get him. And he didn't get me.

Earlier that night we'd snarled at each other because he'd "ordered" me to help serve side dishes to the guests. The male guests. I told him they'd all starve before I fed their male egos or their bellies. The Great Oppressor was not happy with that answer.

So what? If the Great Oppressor didn't want me to turn into a strong woman capable of independent thought, then, hey, he shouldn't have left me in the care of a feminist literary professor. That's all I'm saying.

CNN UPDATE: Grandma JoJo and the Great Oppressor did not get along! JoJo said when my mom gave up her career to pursue "bridedom" it was the saddest day of her life.

Seeds for ugly soap opera sorrow had been sown. The Great Oppressor got his revenge when he made his toast.

He called my mother "his rock" and Amira "his princess." Tipping his iced tea glass in my direction, he said, "Here's to my oldest daughter, Captain Smarty Pants. She proudly carries one of my family's strongest features—the family butt." Everyone laughed.

Oh, yuck, yuck. Quick! Somebody get BET on the phone. Looks like Comicview is missing a star.

Mom gave him a quick shot in the arm that he pretended hurt. My spine remained supple. Inner calm was mine. I would not be rattled.

At least, that was what I thought.

But the Great Oppressor wasn't finished.

He disappeared inside for a second. Croaking frogs in the distance sang a chorus that didn't quite harmonize with the jazz playing from Father's iPod.

He returned to the yard carrying a tray. He walked around the pool and told his brother, my Uncle Ray, to cut off the music. Something was happening.

I drew in a deep breath and inhaled the salty, tangy scent of ripened mangoes and the lush scent of purple bougainvillea climbing lazily over the back fence.

The Great Oppressor dropped to one knee in front of my mother.

He said:

"I was waiting for Mama to get here, but since she called and said she wouldn't make it 'til tomorrow, I'll go ahead." His mother. My *other* grandmother. She was no Grandma JoJo, that's for sure.

He cleared his throat.

"Alicia, you have filled our home with love. You have filled our lives with joy. You have taken my ordinary life and made it extraordinary.

"When we got engaged the first time, I was so poor that I couldn't even buy you a ring. . . ."

Then my mother held up her hand, once again showing the tacky candy machine ring my father had given her almost twenty years ago.

And like always, just the sight of that ring made me cringe. When an otherwise sane and ambitious woman can be lured from a promising career with ten-cent jewelry, well, I gotta think there's a flaw in the system, right? That's what JoJo used to say all the time.

Just to torture the Great Oppressor, I sometimes told him that I planned to have lovers but no husband, and when I got pregnant, I would shoo the man away and raise my illegitimate babies in a cabin in the woods. Maybe start an organic farm and sell apples at a nearby flea market.

The Great Oppressor pulled away a raspberry-colored napkin to reveal a small black velvet box. A pear-shaped teardrop instantly twinkled on my mother's cheek.

He raised his head, then looked up and took her hand and thrust the ring forward.

Watching him look all humble like that, so vulnerable, I can't explain it. My throat felt tight.

"I . . . ," he stammered. He cleared his throat. Nervous laughter and the tense, sweet pull of anticipation tugged us all.

He started over. "Baby, will you marry me . . . again?"

Everyone applauded. All except Aunt Linda—and me. Aunt Linda, my mother's sister, looked like she might hurl herself into the pool out of sheer disgust. She looked so angry.

Immediately I wondered if I looked that way, too.

Great Oppressor, uh, Father, gently put the ring on Mom's finger. It was *ju-mongous*! Huge!

And real.

At any moment I expected fireworks to explode behind their heads in the inky evening sky to elevate the hokey factor yet another notch.

It was hard not to smile because they both looked so happy. So crazy-in-love happy.

Would JoJo have been proud of Mom tonight? Maybe accept my father a little more? Father couldn't help that he was a man and therefore expected women to hand him the universe and keep it clean and filled with folded laundry and hot food.

But my warm-and-fuzzies were destroyed by a single, insensitive Kodak moment. Uncle Ray was popping off pictures left and right. He said, "Man, let me get a shot of you with your beautiful family."

My father swept my mother up and pulled Amira into him with his other arm. Mom held up her hand and wriggled her new five-pound diamond at Uncle Ray's camera. Father said, "I really am the luckiest man in the world."

Mom kissed one cheek. Amira kissed the other.

Teeth flashed. Cameras flashed. Frogs croaked. And I realized:

They made a beautiful family together. The three of them, cocoa brown skin, wide, expressive eyes, huge smiles.

Together, they were the perfect family picture.

Without me.

And no one even realized that I wasn't in the picture.

I should've raised all kinds of commotion. I should have made them include me.

I should have . . .

But I didn't.

WHEN CHARIOTS COLLIDE:

As subtle as Marie Antoinette at a cake tasting, Grandma No. 2 butts in; Kayla bugs out!

CRASH!

It was a quarter past six in the morning, and our house felt like it had been shaken.

Metal sounds. Scraping wood. Did I mention that it was just past **SIX IN THE MORNING?**

Then, nothing.

No screams.

No cries.

Now, this will tell you what a beyond freakish family we are.

Our house just shook like an earthquake that took a wrong turn and woke up under Florida.

And you know the first words out of my father's mouth?

"Mama! Is that you?"

No shouts or shrieks of panic. Just the simple, matter-of-fact statement. Once again, my grandmother, so refined and old-fashioned, had used her tank-sized, environmental hazard of a vehicle to take a chunk out of our garage.

Classic!

I buried my face in the pillow but knew any thoughts of sleep were now just dreams.

Grandma Belle was supposed to be here yesterday. She missed the whole barbecue. Typical. So for the second time, Grandma's large, gas-guzzling, oil-chugging automobile was wedged into the side of our garage. Our front drive curved and the garage sat at an angle.

For Grandma Belle, it was a bad, bad angle.

By the time I dragged through the kitchen and onto the redbrick semi-circular drive, Father Dearest was pulling her from the rubble.

"Mama!" he groaned. Captain Dean, my big, bad, G.I. Joe father, at least six feet, four inches. All muscle.

But let dear Grandma Belle show up, and Captain Commando was more like Private Pillsbury Dough Dad.

"Mama," he said, almost in a whine. "Are you all right?"

She glided from the heap of metal. The front-end of her car, which struck the cobblestone façade of our garage, drooped, making the side of the car appear to smirk. Grandma Belle managed to look fragile, disoriented, prim, and totally in control all at the same time.

"Oh, I declare, I just don't know what is to be done about that silly old garage," she said. "William, are you sure it isn't in the wrong place? Maybe you should have your fellow Army Corps of engineers help you move it just a tad over that way." She pointed and waggled her delicate fingers. Then she re-arranged her hat and said, "I don't know why you had to build your house in the trees, anyway. Not proper, dear."

My arms wrapped around me. I walked out toward the street and looked at the house. It was kind of shadowy. "Maybe you need better light out here," I said.

"Maybe I don't," he growled. Oh, in case I forget to men-tion it later, me giving any kind of advice or suggesting anything to the Great Oppressor sends him spiraling. Says I think I'm a genius.

No, not me. Just Broward County, the state of Florida, and a 4.5 GPA. I fought back a laugh. Besides, I couldn't let him know I disagreed with his mother. I loved that he'd had our house built like a grand tree house. It felt like we were isolated in the woods despite being minutes from the highway.

"Grammy Belle," Amira said, rubbing her eyes.

"My goodness, my dear, you get more and more beautiful each time I see you!" She held Amira out at arm's length and surveyed her body. "You're filling out just fine."

Demolition Diva—that was my name for "Grammy Belle"—looked at me and blinked twice. I cleared my throat and said, "Good morning, *Grandmother*."

"Oh, come here, child. You are always so very formal with your dear, old grand-ma-ma."

Right on cue, she held me in front of her the same way she'd done with Amira.

"Oh, Kayla, Kayla, Kayla. My dear, you're getting to be a young woman. Soon we'll be marrying you off." *Ewww!*

Before I had time to shiver, she added with a cluck, "But the hair. Oh, my! It is a bush, dear. A wild, wild bush!"

It had always galled me and JoJo, too, I think, that even though I spent so much time with JoJo, I looked nothing like her. I looked like Demolition Diva's side of the family. JoJo once said, "Baby, your connection to those people is unmistakable!"

Undeniably, we shared the family butt. My soft brown complexion, button-like nose, and wide smile could have been plucked right off the Diva's face.

Inside I started the coffee. Mother got eggs from the fridge. Amira disappeared down the hall. And Father sputtered, "Are you sure you're not hurt?" and "Can I get you something?" and "Are you thirsty? Hungry? Why don't you lie down for a while and rest?"

She shooed him away. "William, I am leaving for a seven-day cruise on Saturday. I'll have plenty of time to rest. I am fine, my love."

Then she turned in my direction and I froze.

"My church sister, Irene, has a grandson about your age. I've told her we should get you two together," she said. She paused, cocked her head to one side, then added, "But first we're going to have to do something with your hair. Tsk, tsk, tsk, oh, Kayla. Let us not forget, even though you've spent most of your life in Florida"—she said "Florida" like it was some sort of disease—"you were, after all, born in Georgia. You are a woman of the South."

Gulp!

My father grew up outside of Atlanta, and Grammy Belle liked to think she was the hottest thing in the city since Sherman burned it down in the Civil War. She went on, "And you're not still wearing those rummage sale clothes, are you?"

"I wear resale clothes, Grandmother, because I refuse to get caught up in fashion trends. You know, my friend Rosalie's mom says the entire retail industry is designed to get women to compete with one another based on a totally unrealistic and, may I add, unhealthy beauty ideal."

Hmph!

I flinched, hoping hypocrite lightning didn't zigzag out of the sky and burn me to a crisp. Truth was now that I was getting ready to go to Royal Palm, I'd been thinking, maybe being a little bit in style wouldn't be such a bad thing.

Demolition Diva was undeterred. She said, "Oh, that Dr. X person is just a rabble-rouser. I'll bet she doesn't even shave under her arms." The way she pulled her shoulders back and shuddered, you just knew that in her universe, unshaven female armpits were punishable by death.

"Kayla," Grand-ma-ma said, staring at my head, "dear, you're going to have to do something with that bush." Since I stopped getting a relaxer a few years ago, my afro had been kinky and curly and, well, let's face it, unruly.

I had envisioned that with my afro, I'd come across like some retro, butt-kicking version of the seventies icon Pam Grier.

Instead of Foxy Brown, I was more like Frizzy Brown.

Amira had spent most of her young life traipsing around

27

the jungles of Africa with our parents. She had lived in huts and slept beneath mosquito nets. Yet, somehow, she came back here the crown princess of Europe with her relaxer-straight hair.

Really, I don't get it.

My mom, no doubt discerning that a sensitive border was being breached, placed her hand on my shoulder. In a voice too full of gung-ho-ness, she said, "Kayla is just fine the way she is. If she wants to wear retro clothing, she can. Retro is chic, you know? And her hair . . . her hair is fine." I looked at Mom, who looked like telling that lie was about as easy as swallowing her grapefruit whole.

Demolition Diva was not impressed. "She's a good size now, that's for sure. All that gymnastics has built up muscles in her legs and backside. She's thick, but she's solid!"

My face went flame hot. *What am I? National Velvet?* I stifled the urge to whinny and eat a sugar cube from someone's hand.

"Here's what we'll do," the intrepid D-squared went on. "We'll go together this afternoon and get our hair done!"

She smiled her Southern belle smile. My head whipped around. I looked at Mom. **"HELP ME!"** my eyes pleaded.

"Mother Belle," Mom said. "Perhaps you should rest today. You leave for your cruise in just a few days. You really should pace yourself."

Mom's fake bright voice took on a bit of an edge. As in, Grandma Butinsky was pushing too far.

Demolition Diva started to say something, but thought better of it. She nodded at me, but kept quiet. Score one for Mom!

My smirk of satisfaction froze when Amira burst in holding my cell phone.

We exchanged glares. She shrugged. "It was beeping when I passed your room."

A digital neon ribbon of words flitted across my phone's screen. My stomach lurched.

"Is it true? No, right? You're not actually going to try out for the Lady Lions just to prove they have a bias against . . ."

For the second time in a week, my meager, pitiful life flashed before my eyes.

". . . against geeks with no boobs."

All eyes turned to face me. I swallowed hard.

"Amira! You have no right getting in my business."

"True or not true?" she pushed on.

I was close enough to snatch my phone from Amira's hands. The damage, however, had already been done.

My father stopped puttering around long enough to give me an amused glance. "The Lady Lions. Those girls who dance at football games and parades and everywhere? You?"

Heat filled my face. "What? You don't think I'm a good enough dancer? You don't have faith that I could do it?"

He snorted. "I've been paying for your gymnastics and dance lessons since you were old enough to walk. Your mother and grandmother thought it was a good way to help you exercise and defeat your asthma."

"I only took dance for two years," I cut in, but just like Rosalie, he steamrolled right along.

". . . I know you have the ability to do it. And I've seen you dance, even though you refused to be in any of the little whatchamacallits. . . ."

"Recitals!" Amira pitched in. Self-satisfied little termite.

"Yeah. You wouldn't even dance in the recitals because you were scared." He actually laughed.

He went on, "No way do I see you doing this, Kayla."

Then the two of us stared at each other. See, here was the thing about my father: He hated the fact that I was such a loser. His favorite story to tell is about an incident that happened when I was like five or six. Some boy pushed me off the swing set, so I went to play on the slide. The same boy came over and pushed me again. He says I got up and slugged the boy. He says this with pride.

He says, to his knowledge, that was probably the last time I stood up for myself.

He says I need to stand up for myself more.

He says my friendship with "a dominant personality like Rosalie" is the worst thing ever to happen to me. No doubt he feels that my life would drastically improve if I let a dominant personality like him push me around!

Once again they were all staring. At me. My tiny, ice-blue cell phone felt like lead in my sweaty hand.

I spun around quickly and tried to hurry from the kitchen.

Before I could get away, the Great Oppressor called out, "I'll bet five hundred dollars you don't go through with it."

My mom said, "Enough! This is hardly funny, Bill. Stop goading her like that." She didn't sound happy.

Rewind. I stopped, spun around and stalked back. "No, Mom, let him!" I said. The Great Oppressor was kneeling behind a row of cabinets, an impish grin on his face. He looked up at me.

First he looked amused; then he hit me with his cold, hard dare-glare.

So I dare-glared him right back. (I not only inherited my butt from his side of the family, I shared the deadly "dare-glare," too!)

"When I make the squad, I want my money."

Meteor Crashes to Earth;
Radiation Turns Teen Girl
Into Raving Lunatic!

Amira chimed. "Why would you want money? You've got to be the richest person in the family as it is. You're not spending your allowance and holiday money on clothes, that's for sure."

The three of them were trying to keep from laughing. Okay, so I did have a rather large cash reserve. I was thrifty.

After a long exhale, I snatched my gaze from Amira and looked at the Great Oppressor. I repeated: "When I make the squad, I want my money."

He said, "Ten-Four, Captain Smarty Pants, I read you loud and clear. But I tell you what. You don't even have to make the squad. Just make it through the tryouts. Rosalie can't do this for you. She might be able to talk you into it, but . . ."

He stood up, no longer looking up at me, but staring down. I felt humiliated. He was right. Rosalie was my action girl; I was the one always in the background. Did he know that I hated that as much as he did?

"When I make the squad, I want my money. CASH!" My voice sounded foreign.

It was as if I'd been possessed by the Sass Monster. I was on fire.

I shuddered and turned to my mother. "Please, please, please! When I get home I demand DNA testing! He can't be my real father. *Arrrrgh!*"

My gurgled scream was drowned out by the Great Oppressor's parting taunt:

"Take as many DNA tests as you want, but you can't deny the resemblance. You're a lighter shade of brown, but you still have the family butt!"

FROM: ladygodiva
TO: dragonslayer/

feel really bad

FROM: dragonslayer
TO: ladygodiva/

what did u do?

FROM: ladygodvia
TO: dragonslayer/

After bar-b-cue from hell, Mom came in with the tea set.

Wanted to talk.

FROM: dragonslayer
TO: ladygodiva/

(shiver) not the tea set!!!

what happened?

FROM: ladygodiva
TO: dragonslayer/

By the way, my father proposed to her. And instead of seeing it as a way out, she agreed to remarry him.

UGH!

The wedding is in the fall on their anniversary.

FROM: dragonslayer
TO: ladygodiva/

Horrifically pagan; if she wears the big white dress you have the right to run away!

FROM: ladygodiva
TO: dragonslayer/

She saw postcard from Books 'n' Books . . . JoJo put us on their mailing list. We were supposed to go and buy my first first-edition. For my birthday.

FROM: dragonslayer
TO: ladygodiva/

JoJo really believed that when she turned fifteen and bought that first edition, it changed her life, didn't she?

FROM: ladygodiva
TO: dragonslayer/

She said holding that precious old copy of Harper Lee's "To Kill A Mockingbird" made her feel like once and for all she knew what she wanted to do. What she had to do. It was like the old book was telling her to teach. It was a little corny, but it was important to her for me to have that symbol of . . . I don't know . . . my destiny?

FROM: dragonslayer
TO: ladygodiva/

What first edition did she want for you?

FROM: ladygodiva
TO: dragonslayer/

We spent months looking for it . . . she convinced the bookstore owner, an old friend, to help search. JoJo died before Liz found it. That's what the postcard was all about. She found the first edition and is holding. JoJo already paid for it. *Emma* by Jane Austen.

FROM: dragonslayer
TO: ladygodiva

"I do not want people to be agreeable, as it saves me the trouble of liking them." JA

FROM: ladygodiva
TO: dragonslayer/

"Why not seize the pleasure at once, how often is happiness destroyed by preparation, foolish preparations." JA

REBEL WITH A CARTWHEEL:

Elizabeth Cady Stanton and Lucretia Mott sparked a revolution for women voters. Can Kayla dance and flip her way into a new high school world order, or will she and Rosalie lose the vote of confidence?

Let woman receive encouragement for the proper cultivation of all her
powers, as that she may enter profitably into the active business of life.
— *Lucretia Mott*

Here it is. The timeline to the most disturbing, yet amazing day. EVER!

9:07 AM

At dance tryout registration. Rosalie and a few girls from SPEAK showed up for support. Rosalie looked at the unitard and said: "Just like I thought: It's perfect, Kayla, really. You look even flatter than the first time you tried it on."

9:14 AM

Turned in registration card outside the gym. Black construction paper covered the small windows. Apparently tryouts were secret on par with selection of new Pope or winning bake-off

recipe. Two Lady Lions at table stopped talking, took card, then they gave me a long, slow look. Silently they exchanged looks, pointed to an area farther down where dozens of girls were waiting.

9:15 AM

HOLY SWEET MOTHER OF PEARL. I counted one, two, three, four, five . . . one million girls. Apparently tryouts attracted every girl over the age of ten with a bus pass and a dream.

9:16 AM

Secret weapon. My dancing shoes. Sleek, leather Saucony sneakers, white on white. I added lavender laces. With SPEAK we encouraged one another to avoid blatant commercialism and be conscious consumers. And that wasn't just something I went along with to please Rosalie, either. I actually came up with that as a mission. Still, shoes were my weakness. And I'd been saving the Sauconys for something special. . . .

9:36 AM

Hell lost one of its disciples, for she was among us. Mena recognized me from our good ol' days at Flamingo Park, and said: "You've got to be kidding, right? You can't even talk above a whisper without almost wetting yourself. You? A dancer?"

10:45 AM

First round of cuts. I made it. So did forty-nine other girls. Still . . . I was sort of feeling okay. (How's that for enthusiasm?)

11:12 AM

Rest break. We'd been broken into groups. I did all right. Rosa-lie gave me thumbs-up sign. Needed to pee bad. In my haste, **I WENT INTO THE BOYS' BATHROOM by mistake.**

11:13 AM

Burned into my corneas. Saw a real, live penis for the second time in my life. First time happened when I was three. Walked in on Father. Told him, "I don't know what that is, but I think you've broken it." That story was told at family gatherings for the next ten years. Still, that shame can't compare to this. "Sorry!" I shrieked. The boy, the one with the penis, whipped around, he was so stunned to have a girl in the boys' bathroom. Omigod! Then I really, really, really saw it. And I *really, really, really, really, really* wish I hadn't.

11:14 AM

In haste to rush away from Penis Boy, **SMACK!** Door slammed into my face. Everything went darker than last night's stormy sky.

11:21 AM

Came to with Miss Lavender, the dance team supervisor, rub-bing my hand. Others giggling and whispering, "What was she doing in the boys' bathroom. Is she some kind of perv? Maybe she's a transvestite?" I tried to black out again, but couldn't.

12:33 PM

Wanted to just give up and go home. Why not? I'll tell you why not . . . no way was I going to give my father the satisfaction. Take that!

1:04 PM

Time for second round cuts. Oh no, a wedgie. A super, mondo wedgie. Chosen to dance with Group One, I tried to remove wedgie. Girl beside me hissed: "For goodness sake, stop digging in your butt!" *Groan, groan, groan.*

1:07 PM

Routine over. Panted for air in hallway as we waited to see who would be asked back for second day of tryouts. A Lady Lion came over and patted me on the back. "You're really athletic," she said. She left, then someone else tapped me. "You are really good. Good luck." I turned. Found myself eye-to-eye with him. Penis Boy. *Don't look down. Don't look down. Don't look down.* That was all I kept thinking.

1:08 PM

Just realized something. "Penis Boy" was actually the secret crush/love of my life. Penis Boy was Roger Lee Brown. Since I was in kindergarten and he was in first grade and he triumphantly swallowed a bug. Somewhere inside me, I was both grossed out and in love. He was beautiful. He was older. He probably didn't know I was alive. At least, until now. I need a support group. "Hi, my name is Kayla. And I saw Roger Lee Brown's penis."

1:10 PM

I closed my eyes and prayed. Only God could help me now.

2:00 PM

Left gym. We were led out to practice field. "Even though we let you practice and did the prelims inside," said one of the Lionesses, "we also want to see how you perform in front of a crowd." Sun was murder. Seeing spots kept me from focusing on the faces in the crowd. Mouth felt dry. Heart was pounding. I was going to drop dead of either exhaustion or fear. While I waited for death, I danced. Time to pick the finalists. Rosalie came and whispered, "Pay attention. You'll want as many details as possible for your undercover journalism piece when you write about how they dumped you without a second glance!" Glee foamed in the corners of her mouth. I wondered if she wanted that detail chronicled, too.

2:07 PM

A dance team member stood on a concrete wall. She used a megaphone and called out the numbers that were pinned to our backs to let us know who would stay and who would go. If she called your number, you were supposed to come back on Thursday. "Six . . ." No pressure. I'm not nervous. "Twenty-three . . ." Doesn't really matter. "Fifteen . . ." Oh God, if she doesn't call my number I might hurl. "Thirty-three . . ." I wonder how hard it would be to transfer to school in Mexico. My Spanish is muy bueno. "Zero-two . . ." Omigod! Omigod! That's my number. Omigod! Omigod! SHE CALLED MY NUMBER! Rachel Glad, one of the team captains, came over and said, "Girl, you are good. Excellent flips. You look good with the precision stuff, but your hip-hop needs work. Anyway, congratulations. You'll get a call explaining exactly what you'll need to know for your next tryout." Joy started somewhere in my knees and exploded in the pit of my stomach. Joy was short-lived. Rachel continued, "Oh, two things: You won't be able to wear that sweatshirt to the finals." She wrinkled her nose as she pointed to the floppy gray top I'd worn to cover the unitard. "And if you make it, baby girl, we've gotta do something with that hair. Your gymnastics skills are on point. But, um, boo, no, no, no, not the hair. We have to do something with that bush."

2:14 PM
Grandma Belle's words replayed in my mind. *Groan, groan, groan.* Rachel Glad, lead Lion, just sided with Demolition Diva. Bad sign. Bad, bad sign.

SPEAK

Because girls really do have something to say!

"*Ladies, we have lift-off!*" Emma said.

We were at Headquarters. Rosalie's house. Her den, to be precise, with its walls lined with bookshelves filled with every kind of Afrocentric, female-focused book, pamphlet, artifact, and memorabilia imaginable. Her mother, Dr. X, was a self-proclaimed renaissance woman, having written one book that JoJo said was barely readable but that Dr. X asserted was the "rules" for strong, independent women.

And Emma, a longtime SPEAK member, had just helped the group reach another milestone—an official, professional-looking Web page.

The graphics were *gyroscopic wow*—that means filled with color, movement and lots of "BAM!" power. One minute the screen was blank. Next, tiny black letters, all lowercase, spelled "speak" horizontally on the page.

"Honey, that's awesome!" Dr. X said. Emma's face turned pinker than usual. Her green eyes were locked on the screen. Then the screen was like—

Bam!

And the S flipped over.

Bam! Then the P.

Bam! Bam! Bam! E-A-K.

SPEAK appeared vertical once the letters rearranged themselves. At the bottom of the page, the smaller type read:

girls have something to say.

I got a little choked up. First, I got to do a victory dance in my kitchen as my father counted out my five hundred dollars; now I was witnessing a real growth in the club I'd started.

I thought maybe SPEAK should have a chant or a theme song or something. But we didn't, so I just said, "This looks so cool." Inadequate, but heartfelt. I was totally trippin' off of how put-together and . . . real the Web page made SPEAK feel.

Emma tilted her head, and her two Twizzler-like braids fell away from her face. She said, "When the meeting is over today, if we have information about the upcoming 'Kick the Crown' event, we can post it right on the site.'

She clicked an icon of a pair of old combat boots, remarkably like the pair Rosalie was wearing, swinging happily back and forth, kicking a crown. Above and just right of the monitor, Rosalie's face glowed, and ever so slightly her head grew bigger and bigger and . . .

At lunch, Dr. X served turkey sandwiches. Rosalie did her thing.

Her "thing" was to give assignments. My assignment was to double-check with the park about the pavilion. "Will do!" I said earnestly. That was the best way to handle Rosalie when she was in her mode.

Then she went on. "Brewer, I want you to check with your aunt at the radio station. . . ."

"Cousin," said Brewer.

Brewer didn't understand about flow. "Huh?" Rosalie said, frowning.

"I don't have an aunt at the radio station. She's my cousin. Well, actually she is married to my cousin. Lourdes Morales on—"

"All right, your cousin," Rosalie said, exasperated, tapping her icon-like combat boots against the hardwood floor like a gavel. "Your cousin." She emphasized *cousin*. "Make sure she is still going to give 'Kick the Crown' a mention on the air."

Then Tisha threw another monkey-wrench into Rosalie's flow:

"I'm surprised you'd want 'Kick the Crown' promoted on a hip-hop station, considering how misogynistic most of the lyrics of the songs are that they play," Tisha said. Tisha, I'm afraid, has no personality. Day by day, what I see is a girl morphing into Rosalie's mini-me. More and more she's not so much Tisha as Rosalisha.

Scary. I felt like if I wasn't careful, that could happen to me, too.

Tisha's attack on hip-hop led to about a twenty-minute digression on the state of popular music and the fall of modern society.

Finally, the mini-caucus on music ended, and we got back to the main topic—"Kick the Crown."

With Emma on the keyboard, here's what we added to the site:

GIRLS DO NOT HAVE TO BE PRINCESSES TO BE SPECIAL
ARE YOU TIRED OF THE FAIRY-TALE HYPE?
READY TO KICK THE FAIRY-TALE AWAY
TO NEVER-NEVER-AGAIN LAND?

JOIN SPEAK for another women-empowering, awe-inspiring event **Tuesday, August 2 from 1 p.m. to 5 p.m.** at Ocean Side Park in Fort Lauderdale, Pavilion Six.

"Kick the Crown" will feature girls from summer camps all over Broward County. SPEAK will provide guest speakers, give away free stuff, and discuss books, academics, and extracurricular activities that help strengthen girls.

Our goal: To help you find your voice and show that even if you don't look like a disproportionately drawn cartoon character wearing a silly crown you are still worthy, still valued, still capable of being heard.

I got goose pimples when I read it. So what if I had been the one to write it.

"'Kay. Looks good," Rosalie whispered. I nodded.

She squeezed my hand, still whispering. "Just wait. First 'Kick the Crown.' Then your tell-all story about those she-devil Lady Lions. SPEAK will rule the campus in no time."

. . . and bigger and bigger . . . little by little, her head continued to grow.

FLIPPED OUT

Kayla's confidence takes a tumble.

Rosalie and Brewer met me at the gym where I've taken gymnastics since I was four.

I needed to practice for tryouts, Round 2. As usual, Rosalie was having a conniption.

"They are evil troll dolls, that's all. They are wicked!" Rosalie snarled as she held the talc I needed to powder my hands.

I was trying to explain that waiting to tell us about our routines didn't necessarily make them "evil."

"They have narrowed the field to thirty-two girls. Only six of us are going to make it. They're breaking us into groups, and each group has to remember a different dance combination. They just want the competition fair for all of us."

"Us?" Rosalie said. "Us, *chica*? I know you're not really

thinking that those skanks would actually let you on their precious squad."

Ouch! Direct hit!

I tried ignoring Rosalie and focusing on the atmosphere in the gym. On practice days, like today, the gym was loud. Electric. I felt it. Back when I competed, coming to the gym meant letting loose all the feelings I kept bottled up because I was too shy or terrified to speak my mind. Here I could run wild. Run hard. Sweat. Grunt.

Here I was free.

"Excuse me! Hello? Kayla, are you in there?"

Until today.

"Yeah, I mean . . . I hear you," I said.

Then she got all neck-swivelly with her hand on her hip. *Ugh!* "Listen to me, *chica.* Remember this tryout was *my* idea. You're doing this because I said so, OKAY?"

I was blinking rapidly like a gecko in the sun. She had some nerve!

She rolled on:

"Look, you did a good job, *chica.* No doubt. But let's not get it twisted. The Lady Lions are the enemy."

Before I could stop myself, I blurted, "Why, Rosalie? Why are they all of a sudden the enemy?"

Just saying it, confronting her like that, brought an instant stab of something . . . pain/regret/fear/relief . . . something.

As usual, at the first sign of confrontation, I felt my knees wobble, and my internal panic button blared, *Run! Run! Run!* Not Rosalie. Confrontation was like vitamins for Rosalie.

"Oh, no, you did not just ask me **WHY** the Lady Lions are the enemy. I mean, you didn't, right? Not even you could be so naïve."

"Rosalie!" My voice sounded more like a whine than the warning tone I was shooting for.

"Uh, uh, uh! Shh! Just because they smile in your face and pay you a few tired little compliments; just because they had the good sense not to cut you after one day lest they make it too easy to show their bias; just because of that, you think you have a real chance? You are unbelievable."

What I should have done, right then and there, was to tell her to **TALK TO THE HAND** *sister-girl*! I felt like such a fraud. A phony. I wrote all that great stuff about "Kick the Crown." All that stuff about girls speaking out and being heard.

But I was unable to speak up for myself!

Rosalie gave me this look like she could tell what I was thinking. She was like that. I always used to think it was because we were so close we could read each other's minds.

She said, "Kayla, look. You are a great athlete. A great dancer, even. But we're not like them." She squeezed my upper arm when she said "we."

"But, Rosalie, all I'm saying is when it comes to dancing, I really love it. . . ."

The hand again. She gave *me* the hand! Again!

"Don't go there, *chica*. Please. I enjoy dancing, too. But you wouldn't ever catch me in some short skirt in front of hundreds of people wriggling my hips in folks' faces. Can you imagine

Dr. X at a halftime show with me out there looking like a hoochie mama?"

"I know, but—"

"You are trying out to prove a point. Let's not lose sight of that."

I was silent. Experience had taught me to wait. She was reloading. Readying her kill shot. I braced myself. A smarter girl might run for cover, but I just stood there. A lame duck with a big butt.

"Let's face it, Kayla. You're a cute girl, but you don't have the kind of obvious beauty those Lion girls go for." I gulped and self-consciously pressed my hands down my backside, as if I could smooth it out like misshaped clay. She went on, "You don't even know how to wear makeup."

Then she went for the jugular:

"And look at your hair."

Warning! Warning! Ego down!

My fingers shot up to my hair and a sick, burning feeling bubbled in my stomach. I never really thought that Rosalie—ROSALIE—of all people would be judging me based on my appearance. Rosalie in her old faded T-shirts, granny skirts, and combat boots. Well, I guess we can't all be thrift-store goddesses like her!

Having crushed me under her heel like a palmetto bug on the sidewalk, yet totally unfazed or unaware, she reached out and hugged me. I was ego road-kill and she'd just splattered me on the pavement in her tank. Then here she comes, hugging me, patting me on the back.

"K, just keep thinking about 'Kick the Crown.' We have a really important planning session. . . ."

She went on about the planning session. How important it was to make this the best "Kick the Crown" event ever. Like they'd been going on since the early nineteen-hundreds.

Like always, I was too beaten down to put up a fight. I have that in common with many of history's best lackeys.

Deflatamonium.

De-flay-ta-mo-ne-um—when you start out feeling way too good, when you dare to have hope, when your heart is all pumped up, then along comes someone who deflates you at such a rate that the very act of your deflation becomes an event.

Deflatamonium. In spades.

PHOTO FINISH

Kayla races to win distinguished honor of "Life's Most Embarrassing Moment!"

Humilaration.

Deflatamonium is an episode; *humilaration* is a disaster!

Hu-mil-a-ray-shun: the combination of extreme humiliation and frustration. Used in a sentence: *Kayla managed to turn a simple day at home "alone" into an all-time humilaration event.*

Even I can't believe how low I sank today. . . .

I take that back. Sadly, yes, I can believe how low I sank today.

I stayed home to practice my dance routine. Mom and Amira had to take Demolition Diva to do last-minute shopping for her cruise.

My father (since the whole five-hundred-dollar thing, I've

tried really hard to refrain from calling him "the Great Oppressor") had some business to take care of in Miami. That left me. Home. Alone. House to myself.

The deal was this:

A gardener from my father's landscaping business was coming over to do some work so I had to be around to let him into the wild yard behind the tree house—otherwise, the place was mine.

I was still burning up from that whole scene at the gym with Rosalie yesterday. So I'd been practicing hard. I must have done the dance combinations at least a hundred times. No way I didn't have it down pat.

The temperature had to be a hundred and fifty-seven degrees. About a hundred and ten degrees in the shade. And I was steaming. Not because of the heat, though.

Rosalie!

Okay, so at first I wasn't that into being involved with SPEAK or "Kick the Crown" once we got to high school. No more.

Now I wanted SPEAK and "Kick the Crown" to be huge. So I'd come up with my own evil-genius plan, only I hoped my plan would come together as one of sisterhood and fellowship rather than a bloodsport that would pit me and Rosalie against one another like ancient Romans in a pit.

What if I did make the dance team? And then, what if I got the Lady Lions involved with SPEAK? Rather than taking them down, we could work with them to make both groups stronger? Girl power could flourish and my first-person exposé could be about bringing two very different groups together for the common cause of female bonding. How cool would that be?

Maybe the intense, furnace-blast heat had gotten to me. I was thirsty and panting like a shaggy dog. But that was one thing about dancing. Even in my own backyard, all sticky and wet and gross from so much sweat, I felt **GREAT.**

Dance created a Rosalie-safe force field around me. It was like the one thing I had, my superpower, that she couldn't penetrate.

Even so, Rosalie's voice crawled in my head. "Blah, blah, blah . . . they'll never pick you . . . blah, blah, blah . . . you don't have the obvious beauty they're looking for. . . ."

And every time, my heart hammered.

All the feelings, all the words that wouldn't come out of my mouth, well, their meaning, their intensity, came out of my moves. My feet slapped rapidly against the ground. I made quick twists, turns, dips, kicks, shimmies. Hip-hop dance was the Lady Lions' specialty, but I liked mixing the modern moves with ballet and jazz moves, too. My heart rate had to be about three hundred!

I'd thought about it before, the fact that I used my body to let out feelings I didn't express with words.

No wonder, then, that I was stomping, stabbing the air with pointed arm movements, doing deep-waist, bent-knee hip swivels when the idea hit me.

One of the biggest — and most controversial, according to Rosalie — dance performances of the year for the Lady Lions is the holiday show when they dance, high-step, kick, and even do splits while wearing high-heel shoes.

Oh, yes, it is something to see.

Red high heels, short red satin skirts. Movements as smooth and tight as a new clock.

And ever since the first time I saw them do that, I've wanted to dance like that in hot shoes. Shoes with heels.

Okay, here's the deal. You know how much I love shoes, right? Way back one time when everybody came home for the holidays, Mom had a pair of pumps that I absolutely loved. So I stole them. And whenever I got the chance, I'd prance around in them, dance in them, do flips, whatever.

All right, now we're getting to the heart of the *humilaration*. Close your eyes and picture it:

I was out in the backyard.

Music blasting.

My floppy, floofy 'fro was pulled back with a headband.

My black stretchy shorts had ridden up my butt, forming a wedgie that quite possibly might require surgical extraction, and my oversized top flopped down, almost covering all of my shorts.

And I was wearing three-inch, hot pink leather pumps with licorice-black piping and a skinny black bow.

And I was dancing, rolling my hips, shaking my butt—
". . . Front, back, now turn, now turn. . . ." I was jamming.

Then came the big finale.

The big finish.

I took off. All I could hear was my heart beating to the

throbbing bass of the early nineties dance party music. (I'd downloaded it from the Internet.)

Running for all it was worth, I sprang into the air.

One cartwheel.

Two cartwheels.

Then a roundoff. That's a cartwheel where you bring your feet together in the air and nail a flat-footed landing.

And I topped it all off with a split!

Yes!

Kayla Earns Olympic Gold in Hip-Hop Dance
Not Since Wilma Rudolph Has an Athlete Delivered Such a Ground-Breaking Performance;
Women Applaud Worldwide

I'd nailed it. That was the routine I wanted to do. The Lady Lions would freak. And without saying a word, this would be my way of telling Rosalie to talk to the hand, *Okaaaaaay?*

I pumped my fist. I couldn't remember ever feeling so good, not even when I'd won medals at the spring meets.

This was my routine.

This time it was me, not Rosalie, who was the Warrior Princess.

At least, that was how I felt up until the music stopped.

That's when I heard the sound of two hands clapping.

He was standing there, half leaning against the gate, inside our backyard. His arms were folded across his chest all casual and relaxed.

And, much as I didn't want to notice—on account of me being dressed like a stripper, dripping with sweat, and sporting the kind of kinky, floppy, unkempt-looking hair often associated with homeless women—I couldn't help noticing that HE was gorgeous.

More gorgeous than Roger Lee Brown.

Just so you know, Roger Lee Brown is the standard, the measuring stick, but this guy . . . *blind-sexy. Blind-sexy* is somebody who looks so good even a blind girl would go, "Mmm, mmm, mmm!"

"Outstanding." That's what he said to me.

For a full two seconds, I just sat there, still in my split. Then it was like somebody poured hot ants all over my body. Every part of my skin started to tingle and burn. A literal rash of shame broke out. I snatched myself off the ground as though being yanked by the jaws of life.

Before the second downbeat of the next song could shake the air, I stabbed the STOP button on the CD player.

He was still leaning all casual/cool against the fence. Slowly he let his eyes travel from the top of my head to the pointed tips of my mother's pumps. Tiny chill bumps sprang up along my sweaty arms, bare thighs, and grass-encrusted legs. It was like everywhere his eyes touched, my skin got warm, then hot and—not itchy . . . tingly. Had the rash of shame mutated? Gone viral?

And just so you know, in my mind, I'd always told myself that if a boy ever gave me the once-over like that, I'd give him a piece of my mind. Well, at that moment, in real life, me giving him a sassy tongue lashing was *soooo* not about to happen.

When he finished looking me up and down, he brought his gaze even with mine. The whole looking-me-in-the-eye thing was even more unnerving than the way he'd tickled my skin with his stare.

He gave me this sort of half head bob, a gesture thing guys do when they're too cool to actually say "hello."

"W-What's up?" I sputtered.

He shrugged in reply to my lame question. He said, "What's up with you?"

"Huh?"

"I'm Victor Milian. You Kayla?"

Because I'd lost the power to speak, I contemplated sign language. I just nodded dumbly.

"The plants? Your dad sent me."

He had moved away from his slouched stance at the gate. When he stopped in front of me, a backpack full of gardening tools slung over his shoulder, I spun around, got all fidgety like I was making up another kind of dance, then tromped off to another part of the yard. I could feel his eyes following me.

The smell of wet dirt and fruit ripening in the trees mixed with the scent of chlorine from the pool, all combining to make me a little drunk.

He was Hispanic, but dark, maybe Dominican or Panamanian. His hair was shiny and black. His eyes were a deep, dark chocolate brown—large, yet with a sleepy, dreamy look.

Gorgeous.

"Um, yeah, Kayla. I'm . . . I'm . . . Kayla. See, I don't do this. . . . I mean. No. Not all the time. I'm practicing. . . . I'm an intellectual."

Omigod! Did I really just say that? Out loud?

I prayed that the gator reportedly lurking in our area would come loping out of the bushes and swallow me like the loser-kabob I was.

He bent down in front of me and, as his head disappeared from my line of sight, I shut my eyes and tried to magically "vanish" my wide hips.

"Um, Kayla . . ."

He had this voice. It was husky, gravelly, with just a trace of a Spanish accent.

Is that drool I feel on my lips?

When I looked down, he was looking up at me. He smiled and repeated my name. Then I got noodle-kneed and folded until I was on my knees, same as him, eye level again.

"Yes . . . ," I said. My hands were trembling. I held my fingers together and leaned forward all puppy-pathetic.

Maybe he was going to ask me to marry him.

"You've got a lotta hair, Kayla," he said. He was staring. Suddenly, my head felt huge. **HUGE!**

Then I thought, *The nerve of him.* So I said, "Hmph!" And I gave it big attitude to match the big, poofy hair.

He didn't look fazed. "Lotta hair," he said again. "I like it. It's . . . different."

"I just don't think every girl has to be some super-thin,

cookie-cutter Barbie Doll to feel good about herself. *Puhhhf!*
I'm not supposed to be like everybody else!" It all came out so
fast that when I realized I wasn't just thinking it but actually
saying it, I covered my mouth with both hands.

"Um, Kayla, right? You're in the flowerbed. Your dad wants
me to do some work out here. In the garden."

I looked down.

I was in the rich, black dirt of my father's garden. He was
attaching a nozzle to the water spigot.

His eyes were on me.

"Yes . . . well. . . ," I said. My feet came to life. *And we're*
moving, moving, moving.

I didn't dare look back. Um, well, I had to. I couldn't help
it. One peek. He was still watching.

And he was still **GORGEOUS.**

And my pace quickened.

In the heels.

Bright pink heels with the black leather piping.

And I almost made it to the hard rubberized flooring of the
pool deck.

Almost made it out of the grass.

Almost . . .

The slim heel of the pump sank into the grass.

Slow motion—first I tilted, then felt the suction of my
bare, sweaty foot being pulled free of the snug shoe. I was like
one of those women in old Westerns, shot in the back while
escaping an outlaw. Now falling to a slow, agonizing death.

But faster'n you could say, "Yee-haw!" I sprang up. I'd planted my other foot and leveraged myself to keep from falling all the way down.

Tilting, I stood like that for a full second. But I didn't look back. I couldn't.

Hours later, when I rambled on, just a girl and her blog, I couldn't believe my mind had leapt to the whole "marriage" thing. *Ugh!*

Romantic love is an arcane ideal proliferated by a consumer-driven society in an effort to keep women tethered to the antiquated rules of a patriarchal society.

Marriage and the whole "romantic love" thing—it's a farce. Right?

(Sigh! Did I mention that Victor Milian, gardener of the gods, had the best, most wonderful arms with the tightest, most perfectly shaped muscles in the history of god-like gardeners? Not that I'm the kind of girl to be impressed with that sort of thing. I'm just saying. . . .)

TWO TO TANGO?

Rosalie finds comfort in familiar song and dance; Kayla craves rhythm of a new beat!

It's not the load that breaks you down, it's the way you carry it.
— Lena Horne

"... *Bleeeep! Bleeeep! Bleeeep!*"

The smoke detectors!

It was either early in the morning or the middle of the night. I scrambled out of bed, smelling smoke coming from the hallway.

I was *sooooo* tired. Too tired to be afraid of burning to death. Probably because I was already facing trial by fire.

All night long I'd been having crazy dreams of me at try-outs. Wearing Mom's hot pink shoes. Doing my routine. And seeing Rosalie dressed like a female Viking Warrior sitting on a big white horse and holding a flaming sword, while Victor Milian, gardener to the gods, is feeding her steed.

What do you think a dream like that means?

Seconds later Father swept me along, pulling me under his arm. Part of me wanted to protest. I'm not an invalid. I'm not too stupid to find the way out just because I happen to be a girl.

I wanted to say it.

But I didn't.

He was dragging Amira under his other arm with Mom running behind us. "Gotta double-time it, ladies," said Father. He was speaking in military again.

In no time we were out the back door. The not-quite-cool night air felt good on my face. I coughed a few times. Amira, still sleeping, was laid on a chaise.

Demolition Diva appeared, rambling, "Oh, my goodness' sakes. I never would have thought hanging my unmentionables on the stove could cause such a ruckus." Grandma Belle folded and unfolded her hands.

Father, the military hero, unafraid of a little fire, had rushed inside. Sooty faced and practically growling, he yelled, "It's out!"

I had to cover my mouth with my hands to keep from laughing. I am not a frivolous girl, you know. I don't just go around giggling all willy-nilly.

But truth be told, the whole scene was ridiculous. Here was Demolition Diva, wringing her hands, white nightgown flapping in the breeze. And here comes Father, a fire extinguisher in one hand and what remained of a fried girdle in the other.

"Mama," he said, his voice rough like stones in a barrel. "We have a dryer."

She pulled her housecoat tighter. "Now don't go taking that tone with me, William. I am still your mother," she said.

"Ma!" his voice ground harder and he raised the charred girdle that she'd no doubt *once again* left hanging for too long in front of the oven door. Probably fell asleep. She'd done it before. Never set the kitchen on fire, though. Just the stove.

"Those newfangled doohickeys are murder on my delicates," she snapped.

Translation:

Putting her girdle in the dryer would result in the garment squeezing her enormous butt even tighter.

She snatched the fried undergarment from the tip of Father's finger. I looked at Mom, who also had her hand covering her mouth. She used her free hand to grab my free hand and our fingers laced.

Amira woke up on the lounge chair, snorted, then lay back down. The Diva flounced, and the thick giggle in the back of my throat shot out in spurts. My father gave me a rare murderous look, and I didn't spurt again.

Even so, seeing him so mad made it funnier.

Mom squeezed my fingers again. Father stormed off and my mother and I stood in the backyard practically falling on each other trying to keep from laughing.

Weird.

Not the Diva setting fire to her underwear. Sadly, for us, that was normal. Weird was holding my mother's hand. Her fingers were cool and strong. The madder Father got, the harder Mom squeezed my fingers. I didn't want to let go.

Butterflies **the size of pterodactyls** did back flips in my belly. Demolition Diva, however, looked as expertly styled as ever: Freshly trimmed silver bangs swooped to one side. Her pearls were oh so pearly, and she was her usual composed self. Despite keeping the household up half the night thanks to her char-grilled undergarments, Grandma Belle looked immaculate. She sat across from me at the diner. Breakfast at home was out, of course.

"If only my legs had been a wee bit longer," she had been saying, delicately spreading grape jelly on her English muffin, "I might have been a real dancer!"

She looked at me. "You are very courageous, my dear. Going out there in front of all those beautiful girls with their fine figures. I've seen those young ladies. In my day, the boys would say girls with figures like that were 'stacked like brick houses.' They meant that every 'brick' was where God intended." Toast crumbs mysteriously evaporated in midair, not daring to sprinkle and collect on perfectly painted lips.

Mom said, "Kayla will do wonderfully today! I am so proud of you, baby."

I wanted to tell my mother to please stop talking and to please make my grandmother stop talking, too.

"I would have been ashamed out of my mind to go out there and prance around with these hips," the Diva was saying. She clutched at the strand of pearls around her neck and said, "Well, at least your legs are longer than mine, dear. And you're brave. Very, very brave."

LESTER'S DINER — South Florida says goodbye to Kayla Dean. Kayla, fourteen, was found dead beneath booth no. seven at Lester's Diner in Fort Lauderdale, the victim of lethal shame.

At Kayla's memorial, **Maybelle Laura Dean** remarked, "People may remember Rosa Parks as the face of the civil rights movement. People may remember Jane Adams as the voice of our nation's social services programs. But I want you to remember Mikayla Alicia Dean, my granddaughter, as the Hips of Bravery."

"*Exhale*, **chica.** Your *abuela* is from another era. We cannot let her into your head on such an important day!" Rosalie said as the city bus whisked us away to my doom.

The bus was rattling along when Rosalie hoisted this gimongous book out of her backpack and onto her lap.

Not a book, really.

A magazine. My magazine?

"Is that what I think . . ."

Rosalie and I have certain themes that we've been attached to since, like, forever. They are, in no particular order:

* **Marriage often keeps a woman from her true potential.**
* **Society imposes its ideals on women to suit men.**
* **Literature is our only salvation!**

And our "themes" were pretty obvious when she pulled apart the old, worn, crackling pages of my childhood attempt to launch my own feminist magazine.

Goddess.

Now it was all old and the Elmer's Glue had bubbled on the paper.

Inside was a piece of notebook paper glued to the scrapbook with my in-depth analysis of marriage. Rosalie's mom had rented an old movie that now, of course, has been remade. *The Stepford Wives.*

Anyway, Dr. X let us watch the movie with her. It was about this weird town where all the women except these two friends were like "the perfect" women. They were pretty and dressed up to cook dinner and deferred to their husbands.

Then at the end of the movie, you find out they were robots.

Robots programmed by men.

Dr. X told us the movie was demonstrating how society wants to program all women to think and behave like the Stepford wives. I think that was right around the time I came up with *bubblebot* as a word. So I wrote this article for my magazine about the dangers of marriage. I can't help but laugh. I was eleven. What did I know about marriage?

Rosalie's voice cut into my thoughts. "I just wanted you to see this today, Kayla, because I wanted you to remember. I've been there with you. I'm on your side. I want what you want, you know?"

She stared at me. See, sometimes Rosalie could be like that. Sincere and vulnerable. She looked at me as though my agreeing with her was the most important thing in the world.

I nodded. "Of course I know."

The bus shook. I felt light-headed.

"The Lady Lions are not our friends, Kayla. You are in a position to ask questions, study the process, and write a story that will flip the script on how they look at the popular people. All you have to do is write the truth. Tell how those hypocrites kicked you to the curb because of your breast size and not based on your skills."

She paused, sat up straight. In a soft voice she added, "I didn't mean to hurt your feelings yesterday, Kayla. I didn't. I just want to prepare you for what will happen today. Do you belong with a group like that? Could you really be friends with girls like that? You're not trying out because you're some wannabe. You're trying out because . . ." Her voice was usually so strong and sure.

But every once in a while, like at that moment, she could sound almost fragile, like she was fighting back her tears.

"You're trying out because you care about good women. We don't have to settle for Stepford High, right? We're better than that."

A sick uncertainty bubbled in my stomach. I was scared. If I tried to talk I might hurl.

She did have a point. I'd never look like those girls.

But every time I looked at Rosalie and that old made-up magazine, the stomach bubbles churned like volcanic lava. Rosalie was clinging to that old book like it was her lifeline, her Truth.

When I looked at it . . . I felt embarrassed. Embarrassed like any teenager would if they were forced to look at pictures or yearbooks from middle school. It was so ancient and sad. So two hours ago. Didn't she get that?

Looking at that big book made me feel a million miles away from her. That thing between us was growing. And maybe I was to blame.

She was still the girl we'd promised each other we'd always be.

But me?

. . . pterodactyls, in-coming . . .

In a moment of true desperation, I said, "Have you ever looked at any boy and felt like . . . like . . ."

Right away, she cut me off. "Not Roger Lee Brown again, *chica*? I don't know what you saw when you accidentally stumbled into the boys' bathroom, but I assure you it's not worth changing your values over. Let's leave crushes for girls who don't know any better."

At that moment I wanted to scream. Pound my fists on the windows.

But I am one of those girls with crushes! A girl who wants to fit in! Why can't you see that?

We stood, tugged the cord, and held on as the bus came to a stop. We got off, and Rosalie whispered, "It's going to happen, Kayla. You'll see. Today will change everything. Today is our day!"

PRESIDENT ADDRESSES NATION

"Our nation is proud to honor Kayla Dean, a weapon of mass deconstruction—deconstructing the myth that itty-bitties are doomed to failure!"

Okay, maybe the president didn't announce my amazing news from the White House lawn. Still, what happened today . . .

Astromiraculation.

Really, there's just no other word. Being chosen for the dance team is an act so miraculous that it exceeds the boundaries of Earth and space. *Astromiraculation.*

Of course, the road to *astromiraculation* was filled with oozing clumps of frustration and jagged cliffs of embarrassment.

When I first got to the tryouts, I thought I'd end up in a subterranean grotto of shame and retribution normally reserved for fashion slaves, child abductors, and boy-crazy teen queen wannabes.

Finalists signed in at the performing arts building. We were allowed thirty minutes to stretch and practice. We were being judged in three categories—group dance choreography, individual performance, and gymnastics/freestyle.

Tryouts: 10:04 AM

To ensure the tightest security possible and decrease the chance that some dance-move-stealing mole might infiltrate another girl's tryout, tape her moves with infrared lenses, and hijack a patented double-thrust twirl, we were assigned numbers and then sent to different areas of the two-story building, led by a dance-team guardian.

Paint fumes filled the front entrance, and workers with ladders and other equipment pushed past the girls, up the stairs, and beyond the double fire doors. A Lady Lion with a megaphone, a clipboard, and—I kid you not—a pair of binoculars stood on the top step and scanned faces as we approached. Could Kevlar-vested SWAT teams be on nearby rooftops scanning for terrorists, or worse—the popularity impaired?

Rosalie and all other friends-of-friends were directed to an area beyond the roped-off front entrance.

"This is a total load of crap! These girls are on a complete power trip," roared Rosalie, stomping her foot and otherwise behaving all power-trippy herself. "I can't wait 'til we take them down."

I signed in and was led away, like they suspected I'd spent the night telegraphing sensitive troop movements to a cave in some war-torn country. My "tryout chaperone" and I rounded a corner, and I felt the slithery weirdness of nerves and terror squiggle in my stomach. My knees had begun to shake.

Then a scary encounter. In a near-breach of confidentiality and security, Angeline, the girl entrusted to protect my dance secrets, and I stumbled upon the first finalist to sign in.

"No one else is allowed back here, Angeline! You can't be here!" the girl's chaperone yelled.

"Karla, you're in the wrong place. Look at the map!" Angeline shot back. Neither girl looked ready to give in. Angeline wore tough-looking black leather high-tops. So you just knew she wasn't going to back down.

They both raced over to a notebook tossed casually on the floor and produced a colorful map with the fierceness of government agents battling foreign fashion-label knockoffs. My mind raced back to those emergency distress training days of elementary school. Should I stop-drop-and-roll or hit the floor and cover my head?

I tried to avoid eye contact with the other finalist. Could she look in my eyes and see that my freestyle would be riddled with a combination of flips and spins or that my secret weapon—a swing dance step, in high heels—ended in a back walkover and a split?

Angeline stood, hands on her hips, and blew out a huge sigh. A photo my mother took of a triumphant wildebeest set against the vast skyline of Kenya popped into my head. That wildebeest had looked radiant, masterful after its kill. I knew the black high-tops were not to be played with.

Chaperone One and her charge slunk away in defeat. Angeline turned to me, hands still on her hips. "Well, don't just stand there. You've got thirty minutes, girl. Get it together."

And with that, I began to move to the rhythm pounding in my heart.

Time to dance

Angeline got a call on her cell, then told me I'd be in the first group.

Downstairs, I joined seven other girls onstage. Miss Lavender and four former dancers, all graduates, sat in the front row of the auditorium. All of us looked terrified, and for a moment we were stumbling over one another.

But when the music started, something happened. It was like everything else went out of my head. I just knew what to do. We did the same formation, same steps even though they changed the music three times.

When they were done with us, we were panting—at least, I know I was. But my knees weren't shaking.

When it was over, I was getting up out of a split and the judges, Miss Lavender included, were on their feet applauding.

I couldn't believe it. My freestyle was so down, so on-point, I was afraid I might have to go into some sort of Dancer Protection Program for fear my skills were just too lethal for the rest of the world. I breathed a sigh of relief.

We were all led into the auditorium and we sat in the plush cranberry-red seats while the judges went up to a long table that had been placed on the stage. Janet Jackson's "Pleasure Principle" played in the background. Ah, yes. An old-school ode to dance-team routines worldwide.

They'd debate for a minute, then they'd look at us; debate, then look at us. It was surreal. When my mom was still in the jungle taking pictures of elephants, JoJo would tell me that whenever my heart raced or thumped in my chest, I should think about the rhythm of the African drums. When I was eight or nine, Mom brought home a drum for me for Christmas. She showed me how a tribal elder had taught her to play.

Instinctively, my fingers fluttered over the spot in my chest where my grandmother's words lived and my mother's drum played.

"Are you all right?" the girl next to me asked.

When I looked at her, I felt the itch of tears and blinked several times. Afraid one word might set free a dam, I just nodded.

The girl grabbed my arm and squeezed gently. "You'll be fine. No matter what happens, whether you make it or not, you'll be fine."

I nodded again; then she moved down to another group of girls. She thought I was getting emotional about the tryouts, about making the squad.

Nope. Well, not exactly. I mean, I was nervous, but something in me also felt . . . afraid.

What *would* JoJo think about me doing this? I squeezed my eyes shut and this time felt the warm trickle of a single tear on my cheek. My mother had tried to reassure me the other night, but I chased her away. It was so hard all of a sudden, knowing what was right and what was wrong. What was real and what was surreal.

The drum in my chest played louder, with more intensity. Even the pulse in my neck thumped a beat. So many things were racing through my mind. I was terrified these girls would think my butt was too big or my breasts were too small, even though, according to Rosalie, that was what I was here to prove. Then I was terrified I'd become the kind of girl who cared if other girls thought her butt was too big or breasts were too small.

I was changing, I could feel it. I didn't mention it, didn't want to talk to anyone about it, but I was, I knew I was. And I knew part of the reason I'd been such a witch to my mom was that she could see it.

Even when she'd come to visit, before the cancer quickly overwhelmed JoJo and took her away, Mom noticed. It bothered me that as much as I loved my grandmother, my mother was able to see in me what JoJo could not—that I wanted to be more than books and intellect. That I was getting bored living inside my little box.

And wanting all that change and feeling so much change scared me because holy, sweet mother of pearl, I'd spent my whole life learning how to be the Me that I am. Did I really want to shift gears in high school and start being all brand-new?

Rosalie was downstairs, pacing back and forth, rooting for me to fail so she could see my failure as a victory.

But I knew in my heart, I didn't want to fail. Even if it did mean I wouldn't get the high school story of the century. I wanted to write a different story. One about two groups of girls who seemed to stand for different things, yet became determined to unite in order to make life better for all kinds of girls.

I had to find a way to bring SPEAK and the Lady Lions together. But first I had to find out whether or not the Lady Lions thought I could hang.

"Girls, come forward please. . . ."

And then, just like that, it was over. Girls were shrieking, crying, laughing, squealing. I almost couldn't walk. One girl wailed, screeched, "No, no, no, I can't believe it, no!" She was grabbing me, holding me, pulling me into her misery swirl.

All around me girls stumbled and stammered, hooted and cried out in stages of disbelief like lifetime felons finally set free to see the ocean and run barefoot in the sand.

First I couldn't walk, then I was stumbling, then running. I was part of a herd now. A zebra.

A Lion.

Rosalie and the other FOFs had come un-"penned," leaving the confines of their grassy waiting area and were milling around the cement steps. "I made it!" My voice was so high and shrill that the force of it doubled me over.

Her face was blank. So I screamed again.

"Rosalie! I didn't get cut! I made it! I made it! **I MADE IT!**" This time I dropped to the ground, buried my face in my hands, then sprang up and stamped my feet against the concrete.

Shooting pins of pain and life and magic shot through my ankles. I felt everything and everything felt good.

Crazy glee coated me when I looked up again, looked at Rosalie's face, expectant, you know? Needing her . . . what?

Joy?

But girlfriend had no joy for me. Here I was so huge with joy that I was positively *joygantic*. Not Rosalie.

Her face collapsed like an eighth-grader's science fair volcano left out in the rain. Then her features squenched into a squirmy expression of disbelief and disgust.

"You made it? The Lady Lions are going to let YOU be on their squad? You made it?"

OBITUARY NOTICE: *Joy Is Dead!*

My face got chili pepper hot. Heat — part shame, part "how dare she" anger — made my skin hot. Still, I nodded my head like a fool bobblehead doll. "I made it, Rosalie. I'm . . ."

My voice caught in my throat. A murderous look blazed in her crazy glee-free eyes.

"You what?" she growled.

"Kayla!" — before I could answer, before I could plead — "I'm so happy! Be happy with me!" Several hands came around me and I was swept into a group frenzy. *Joygantic* in a big, big way!

"Can you believe it? We made it?" said the girl who'd comforted me in the auditorium. Then we were all jumping again.

Minutes later, when the jumping and hugging had subsided, I spun to look for Rosalie.

Gone.

Later, I called her from my cell.

No answer.

Hours passed.

Still, no Rosalie.

AMBER ALERT:

Be on the lookout for a missing best friend.

Last seen fleeing the scene of a celebration.

PEARLS OF **WISDOM**

Kayla discovers that love, like a precious gem, is a treasure one only needs to accept.

Rosalie left me hanging all weekend. Can you believe it? She wouldn't answer my calls, pages, e-mails, smoke signals — nothing, then, presto, she is here and ready for action.

Hmph! Allow me to recap the past forty-eight hours of her disappearance:

I'd been helping the Demolition Diva pack her sturdy "delicates" and other necessities for her cruise with the church ladies.

At Port Everglades, where the cruise ships line up awaiting their vacationers, the whole family waved and took pictures and made a big fuss. I must say, Grandma-ma looked so happy in her buttery yellow suit and hat that I couldn't help smiling at her.

That was until she gripped my face in her hands and got,

like, nose to nose with me and said, "Child, I am very, very proud of you. You were so brave to go out there, to throw caution to the wind. You showed 'em what for!"

I wasn't sure whether she was talking about my trying out for and making the dance squad or if she thought I'd swam to Cuba and brought down Fidel Castro's dictatorship.

"Um, thanks, Granny," I said.

She gave my face a small shake. "Don't say 'um,' child. Be steady and sure in your speech. And don't call me 'Granny,' either. 'Granny' is a sour apple, dear."

Even the salty scent of the ocean and the bustling sounds of passengers, car horns, fog horns, and seagulls couldn't totally distract me from the parting shots of my own personal Steel Magnolia.

"Yes, ma'am," I said.

She smiled and looked around dramatically. Then she did the oddest thing. She reached into her bubblegum pink vinyl shoulder bag and pulled out an oblong black velvet box.

A jewelry box.

She handed the box to me. I looked at Mom, then the Great Oppressor, but they both shrugged. Amira managed to scowl and look bored at the same time.

"What's this . . . ?"

"Open it!" Grandma-ma's voice was bright and crinkly, like foil wrapping paper. Inside the box on a padded bed of satin lay a beautiful, perfect strand of pearls. I was so stunned that I dropped the box and the pearls spilled, and for a moment I was paralyzed in horror.

But contrary to her reflexes behind the wheel of her car, my grandmother's reflexes for retrieving runaway jewelry was flawless. In one motion she swooped the pearls from the ground, stepped behind me, and began to unfasten the clasp.

My fingers instantly flew to the strand of pearls, which felt majestic and important on my throat. But it was the pearl of wisdom she left in my ear that gleamed brightest.

When she'd finished with the clasp, she softly whispered in my ear so no one else could hear, "I know how close you were to . . . your grandmother JoJo. I know you miss her. But remember, I am your grandmother, too. Wear the pearls like the lady you are. I'm proud of you."

That was yesterday . . .

Now, a day later, while my grandmother and her church friends were walking on water, I sat in our backyard, biting my lip and running my finger along the crests and valleys of my brand-new pearls. (Yes, I was still wearing them!)

And believe me, with the tear Rosalie was on, I needed the pearls, anything for support. After her little disappearance, she had the nerve to come in here and act all "everything-is-going-according-to-plan."

Ha!

Now she claimed making the squad was the most perfect way for "us" to get our agenda "out there."

"Think about it, K. Before, you would have had a good story, but some heretics would have tried to dismiss you and claim your article was bogus because you were bitter over not making it. Now we don't have to worry about that, do we?"

She was so close to me that when she said it, I could feel her quest for power.

Pebbles of anger lodged in my throat, but uncertainty and maybe fear pressed like a sack of stones on my chest. "But . . ."

Bam! Before I could get more than a word out, she hit me with the palm-up hand in my face.

"No time for that now, Kayla. Right now we have more important things to worry about. Like getting to work on 'Kick the Crown.' We're meeting with some women from the community—the radio stations, one girl from Channel Seven, and Dr. X said she even got a call from a legislator's office. We're meeting with them next week."

The she hit me with a whammy. Telling me she was leaving town in a few days so I was going to need to "step up my game."

Ugh!

"Rosalie, I have practice every day, every minute, almost every hour until school starts."

"So?" she countered. Her level of *funktivity* never wavered. Just so you know the difference—*funktaciousness,* in the book of Kaylaisms, describes boldness, like fashion or a high spirit, but *funktivity,* that's just plan ol' *stankaliciousness* run amok.

"Look, Rosalie . . ."

"Go to the practice, chica, whatever, just . . ." She pulled out a day planner full of phone numbers and of course numerous lists.

"Just follow the lists. Make sure everybody knows where

and when. The planning session's at our house, so you know the drill."

Aye, captain!

Then she reached into her bag and pulled out a small package. It was a slightly wrinkled — recycled — gift bag.

"Here," she said, pushing it at me. I opened it and pulled out a crisp, fresh T-shirt. It read: *This is what a feminist looks like.* When I met her gaze, she shrugged.

"Ordered it on the Internet after you made the squad. I . . . I am proud of you, Kayla. You really did it."

We hugged awkwardly, then just as abruptly as she showed up at my front door, she was gone.

GATOR **BAIT**

Private dance time leaves Kayla mired in a
swamp of humiliation!

Our first practice:

It was well over five hundred degrees. We were outside in
an enclosed field behind the school. We weren't practicing with
the marching band yet. For now we were just working on our
own. All around RPA were scaffolding and tractors and construction equipment, all with growling motors to give the school
a face-lift before the school year started.

After three hours, I was a funky, molten mess. Sadly, heat,
humidity and musty armpits would be the high points of my
afternoon.

Allow me to explain.

First, there was our dance team coordinator, Miss Lavender. Miss Lavender is the stuff of urban legends.

HER VITALS:

✳ superlong legs and razor-thin eyebrows

✳ former professional dancer currently married to a Miami Dolphin football player

✳ rumor has it that she jogs Fort Lauderdale beach in her stilettos

✳ rumor also has it that she periodically trains with the Navy SEALs just to stay in shape

We'd finished, so I dropped into a self-made puddle in the grass. Next thing I knew I was shocked into an upright position as her long, dark shadow stretched across my aching body. Not wearing stilettos. Black leather jazz shoes with a Mary-Jane strap.

Miss Lavender: "You are the youngest member on our squad, Miss Dean. We had quite a bit of discussion about whether or not to select a fourteen-year-old sophomore. We chose you because we felt you'd be able to grow into our system and be a real asset. Not to mention the fact that you blew us away with how you were able to dance and perform in those high heels."

Me: "Um . . ."

Miss Lavender: "But . . ."

Why is it that with me, there's always a "big but"?

". . . What we need to concentrate on now is your confidence. You've got all the moves, but you lack the attitude. You gotta' work it like you mean it."

I scrambled to my feet and started brushing myself off. Then, Roman Nivens, a junior and the quintessential male choreographer of dubious sexual orientation, piped in:

"Girlfriend, you have got to learn to be more at ease with your body." He looked me up and down, his willowy thin arms crisscrossing his chest like ancient snakes from a pharaoh's crypt.

Roman: "Little Diva, I promise, once you start to ooze confidence, you'll have tons of fans, and little girls will want to grow up and be just like you." *Little Diva!* Oh, no he didn't. My family had only one "Diva" and she was of the demolition variety, currently out to sea, thank you very much.

Me: "Um . . . duh."

I stood there blinking like a gecko on a limb. The whole squad was checking me out, no doubt feeling all kinds of pity for the pathetic little sophomore with no makeup and clothes from The Salvation Army. Instinctively, my hands crept around back in a useless, sad attempt to cover my rear end.

Roman appeared to get some sort of signal from beyond because no sooner had my hands slid behind me to cover my butt did he jump forward with a big, fat "Aha. See what I mean. Girl, you better stop trying to cover yourself up. The booty is your friend."

Medic! I need someone to come and pronounce me dead at the scene.

Of course, it got worse, because, well, it could.

Nena Hyde stepped forward. She introduced herself, although I remembered her from tryouts.

"I know you're not self-conscious about your behind, right? Girl, no pun intended, but that's an asset."

Death by utter mortification.

Nena went on, "Don't worry, we've got your back. Honey, anybody who can waltz into one of our tryouts and work a pair of high heels the way you did has to have the Lady Lion attitude in her. We just have to help you pull it out."

Shame and sweat dripped from me, but I could still see that she was one of the most flawless individuals I'd ever known. Nena Hyde was the kind of girl black poets wrote about. Gorgeous. High cheekbones, wide mouth, and intense dark eyes. And unlike mine, her afro had a distinct shape and was held away from her face with an animal print scarf.

Another girl, Evelynne something-or-other, snorted. Without looking at me, she sort of flicked her nails, smirked, and said, "She better get it together 'cause I don't want us to lose ground messing around with somebody with issues."

Nena glanced at the girl and made a little snort of her own. "Ev, please. She won't fail."

She turned and looked right at me. Nena's eyes were dark, almost hypnotic, and her gaze didn't waver. "You won't let me down, will you?"

I swallowed hard. It wasn't a question. My head bobbed up and down automatically.

Miss Lavender declared practice officially over. She patted me on the shoulder and said, "Remember, Kayla, dancing is about more than doing the moves, it's about looking fearless — and fabulous. You were too self-conscious out there today, but you weren't like that at tryouts. If you're concerned with how others are seeing you, don't be. It'll make you crazy. Your confidence, your power, will come from looking inside and trusting yourself. And I think if you just tweaked your look, you'd feel more comfortable."

Right then I wanted to thank her for her encouragement.

I wanted to tell her about SPEAK and how I'd given almost the same speech to a number of grade-school girls when I was in middle school. That's what SPEAK was about. We not only socialized with each other, but we went to grade schools and worked with younger girls to make them feel good about themselves. I wanted to tell Miss Lavender about SPEAK and say a lot of things.

But I didn't.

Instead, my mouth opened, but my words were sliced away by another voice.

"Kayla **IS** comfortable with her body. She's just not used to prancing it around in front of the whole world."

Rosalie!

What was she doing here? She was standing a few feet away, hands jabbed into her hips. Her expression said, "I dare you!"

Miss Lavender's eyebrow arched, and for just a brief second I feared she might go all ninja on Rosalie.

I swallowed hard. "That's my—"

"Best friend," Rosalie finished my sentence, glaring.

Rosalie Hunter vs. the Lions.

It went like this:

Miss Lavender exchanged looks with Roman and Nena.

Nena looked Rosalie up and down, then in a voice so soft that it flowed like liquid, she said, "Well, Best Friend, it's nice to meet you."

Miss Lavender pulled a pair of dark sunglasses out of somewhere, put them on, then told me, "You're a beautiful girl, like all my girls. But you dance like you're trying to hide your body. Dancing is about being seen, so get used to it."

So then Rosalie rolled her eyes way back in her head and made a loud snorting sound. She said, "That's right, Kayla, all the world's problems can be fixed with a booty shake and a makeover. I hear a new look can cure world hunger and end wars, too. Somebody get me Iraq's prime minister on the phone. Peace is just a hair extension away!"

By then my throat was so dry and hot I could've hiccupped and caused a brush fire.

Roman looked sideways at Rosalie and said, "Nice shirt."

When Roman said that thing about Rosalie's shirt, two things happened to me:

I looked at Rosalie. She was wearing a THIS IS WHAT A FEMINIST LOOKS LIKE t-shirt, only it was an old one. We'd gotten them years ago. It didn't fit anymore. Her curly hair was a mess and her shirt was just too tight and too wrong.

Seeing how out of place she looked, I wondered if I looked like that, too.

I got this greasy feeling in the pit of my stomach. I felt so embarrassed. But not for myself. I was embarrassed for Rosalie. She didn't belong.

And maybe I didn't, either, but right then, I knew I wanted to.

Miss Lavender had been leaving, but stopped next to Rosalie, looked over at her then turned to me and said, "Kayla, you're going to have to deal with how people treat you now that you're one of us. Posers will pretend to be your friend, and people you thought were friends all along might become jealous that you've achieved something they could not. Don't let anyone take this away from you, Kayla. You are now officially a Lady Lion. Learn to love it."

And with that, she snapped her fingers, glanced at Rosalie through her way-dark shades, and strutted away. Roman, following close beside her, turned and chimed, "Girl, you can't let haters rule your life." With that, the pair disappeared in a cloud of parking lot dust and attitude.

Rosalie sputtered and spewed out something like, "Oh, please! Like I'd ever lower myself to be a dancing, prancing Lady Lion."

I knew at that moment that the awful, slippery feeling in my belly wasn't just embarrassment. I felt sorry for Rosalie. Pity. *Ugh!* You're not supposed to pity your best friend. But I did. She sounded so . . . so . . . desperate.

Several dancers remained, including Nena and Rachel Glad, but nobody was paying Rosalie any attention.

A girl named Tangie, another new squad member, said, "You've got nice hair. Don't worry, girl. We'll get together and I will hook you up."

Rosalie huffed, "Hey! Are any of you listening? Don't you get it? Kayla's not like you. She has more important things to deal with than the right shade of lip gloss. My best friend doesn't need a *look*!"

"Hey, New Girl, tell your bodyguard over there to get a life," said one dance team member whose name I didn't know yet.

"And a lip wax," chimed another.

Then, turning to each other, the two Lady Lions circled around Rosalie, shaking their heads. Rosalie was like a dying zebra on the African plains. Easy pickins for a couple of lions.

Lioness One:

"Girl, where did she get that shirt?"

Lioness Two:

"The shirt is not the problem. The fact that she's been hanging onto it since kindergarten is the problem!"

Rosalie went rigid. Lionesses One and Two continued to circle.

When Rosalie finally spoke, her lips pulled thin and tight, I felt the air seep out of me. I knew where we were headed, and it wasn't a pretty place.

> " 'My oldest daughter is Nefertiti
> The tears from my birth pains
> created the Nile
> I am a beautiful . . .' "

Groan! Groan! Groan!

She had leapt over any references to her hero, Dr. Condoleezza Rice, and gone straight to "Ego Tripping," a poem by Nikki Giovanni.

One and Two exchanged glances. Rosalie had done this before. Whipping out poetry or literary references to beat down those who would dare oppose her. *Egad!*

With hand on hip and a fierce look in her eyes, Lioness One, complete with shoulder-rocking head movements, said:

> *"'I gazed on the forest and burned*
> *out the Sahara desert*
> *with a packet of goat's meat*
> *and a change of clothes*
> *I crossed it in two hours*
> *I am gazelle so swift . . .'"*

Lioness Two, pressed her cheek against Lioness One's and picked up the flow: "'. . . So swift you can't catch me . . .'"

One and Two exchanged high fives. Rosalie looked as though she had swallowed that packet of "goat's meat."

One said:

"Lest we forget, this is RPA, a school where everybody is an academic star. Don't come over here acting high and mighty just because you've learned a poem. What you need to do is go home, regroup, and don't come back until you're really sure you know what Ms. Giovanni was trying to say!"

Two added:

"And for Lord Jesus' sake, if you're going to carry on about feminism, stop giving the movement a black eye with a shirt too

95

small for my teddy bear!" And with that, she turned, reached into her shoulder bag, and removed a crisp, folded t-shirt identical to the new one Rosalie'd just given me.

She unfurled it to show its length and width, then tossed it right into Rosalie's face. Reflexively, Rosalie caught it. Two said, "Oh, yeah, my aunt is a judge and when she campaigned earlier this year, we 'Lions' worked together on her campaign. See we do that sort of thing when we aren't out shaking our butts, or whatever. We had extras. Wear it in good health, girlfriend!"

And with that, Lionesses One and Two communicated in the international language of eye rolls, a Morse Code of cool. And then they were gone.

"So, Kayla, is this how it's going to be? Are you going to let those girls bully you into being something that you're not?"

My head was pounding. Too much sun, too much dancing, too much Rosalie.

"Rosalie," I hissed. "Enough! Please, you are making a scene."

"A scene!" she roared. "I couldn't possibly be making as much of a scene as you were a few minutes ago. Out there wriggling around. I thought you saw yourself as an *intellectual,*" she said in a singsong, mean way. "I thought you wanted to be a serious journalist and novelist. Oh, yeah. I'm sure Zora Neale Hurston took several breaks when she was writing *Their Eyes Were Watching God* so she could go and shake her butt with the local bands. What kind of legendary woman do you want to be?"

"Rosalie, there are all types of legends. What about Cher? Marilyn Monroe? Queen Latifah?"

"Queen Latifah has never been seen twisting and carrying on the way you were."

Now it was my turn to scream in frustration. Sweat ran from my forehead into my eyes and burned. I thought about yoga. I thought about breathing through my belly button. I tried to picture my calm, happy place. I blew out a breath and tried to start over.

"Rosalie," I said, my tone pleading. The approaching afternoon storm crouched low in the clouds. A downpour was soon to come. Hot and damp, the air hung like body heat. "What if we've held a not-quite-right opinion of them? I mean, maybe they're not—"

"What? Maybe they aren't shallow? Maybe they aren't more interested in appearance than what's inside? You heard them, Kayla. I didn't put words in their mouths. I'm here to remind you not to turn your back on an organization that feeds your soul. And what are they doing? From the lead go-go dancer on down they're trying to pressure you into becoming the next Li'l Kim. While you're getting your lobotomy will you be getting fake boobs?"

What if she is right?

All of a sudden, it started to rain in my happy place and my belly button was gasping for air. I told her I wouldn't let them change me, but she just barked, "Girl, it's already happening. Wake up!"

The others were all gone. Sweet, wet grass smells filled my head as I plopped, exhausted, onto the curb and buried my face in my hands. This was a disaster. How was I going to convince the girls to join SPEAK? They would laugh me out of existence. I exhaled. A few feet behind us the sprinklers had come on. I loved the fresh, almost rustic smell of ground water that came out of sprinklers.

I wanted to be angry. I wanted to fight for myself. But I felt drained. Rosalie dropped down beside me. I asked, "Rosalie, why did you come here?"

When she turned to face me, her expression was yet another dark cloud draped across my day. It was like I was watching her turn into a stranger right in front of my eyes. "Pappy, my grandfather is sick. We're leaving tomorrow for Baltimore." We were both silent.

She was like one of those rainbows you see when the sunlight hits the water dancing in the sprinklers at just the right angle—misty, wondrous, but hard to make out. I wanted to reach out and grab her, pull her to me, and beg her just be my friend.

I need you to be my rainbow!

"You are my best friend, Kayla. Mine. We are best friends. You can't choose them over us!" She stood, loose grass sticking to her legs, and stalked away, shrinking against the drooping clouds.

Despite the heat, I shivered. The sun was gone, and when I looked at the dancing water from the sprinklers, there wasn't a rainbow in sight.

NELLIE BLY OR BIG FAT LIE?

Kayla struggles with journalistic dreams amid
pressure from pushy peers!

Being a reporter seems a ticket out to the world.
—Jacqueline Kennedy Onassis

𝕴 was at the Sunshine Pavilion, the
auditorium for RPA. Almost the same seat I'd waited in while
they deliberated on who'd make the Lady Lions.

Somehow, this time, I was feeling even sicker inside.

Journalism students had gotten a letter about our orientation. The letter stated we had to bring ideas that represented
what we planned to accomplish.

Ugh!

I had only a few minutes before I could decide whether to
announce that my big plan was to expose the inequalities of the
Lady Lions and prove that they discriminate against itty-bitties
such as myself.

A vision of Rosalie, head tossed back, a maniacal laugh

spilling from her mouth, blurred my vision. Dr. Sam Morrison, Dean of the Journalism program, was talking, but with Rosalie's crazy cackle rattling my brain, I could barely hear him.

Focus . . . focus . . . focus!

At first, he asked what we'd been reading for the summer. Panic!

How long had it been since I'd been on listmania, the on-line site where I posted my favorite reads. Grandma JoJo said a serious woman, an intellectual, should always know the literary works that most influence her life. Mine were:

- ✳ *Their Eyes Were Watching God* by Zora Neale Hurston
- ✳ *Emma* by Jane Austen
- ✳ *The Secret Lives of Bees* by Sue Monk Kidd
- ✳ *Speak* by Laurie Halse Anderson
- ✳ *Nellie Bly: Daredevil, Reporter, Feminist* by Brooke Kroeger

Anyway, I was replaying the list in my head and thinking about how I was more than a little bit of a hypocrite since one of my favorite series of all times, *Buffy the Vampire Slayer,* was not part of my listmania selections because it didn't really fit the whole "serious woman" image, when I noticed Dr. Sam's voice went from nurturer to disciplinarian.

"You have to have commitment," he was saying. "You have to have a sense of purpose. Between your classwork, external assignments, and responsibility to your other classes, a lot will be asked of you. Young people, you will have to ask yourselves,

'Am I up to the challenge?' No one can answer that for you except you."

Gulp!

After that it was all downhill—for me, anyway.

NEWS ALERT .´. . Dr. Sam (he'd told us to call him that instead of Dr. Morrison) wanted us to work on an assignment due the first day of class. "If you have a video camera at home, use it. If you don't, come to the school and we'll get you one. Use it. Write a script, a short biographical story, if you will, about what you see as your greatest challenge for the coming year." He said we didn't have to turn in the video but we did have to turn in the script.

Great! Just Great!

THIS JUST IN . . . He wanted to know what wonderful, fabulous, well-thought out gems of journalism we had to offer.

Sheena, an appropriately named girl with shiny hair and black-rimmed glasses, a button nose, and alert brown eyes, edged forward in her seat. "Dr. Sam, I just want to say that I am committed to being in this program."

She smiled.

Dr. Sam smiled.

Maybe the whole friggin' world smiled!

She went on, still flashing her beauty-pageant smile. "I am working on an investigative piece of journalism. I want to know how or if the school system tracks homeless children and whether or not kids whose parents have no homes get discriminated against by the schools."

Another big, BIG smile. Dr. Sam nodded his approval.

More hands went up. "I'm planning to investigate the highly competitive nature of the science fair . . . the football team . . . the solar system . . ." On and on it went, 'til the only one left was . . . me!

They all turned, looked at me.

Sheena, the shiny-haired girl, turned. "Dr. Sam," she said, pointing as though giving testimony from the jury box. "I believe she has not had a turn."

Dr. Sam gave another slight nod, this time at me. He was wearing gold-rimmed glasses and his short hair was dusted with gray along the edges.

"Miss . . ."

"Dean." Not me. Shiny hair was giving my name, speaking when I should've been speaking. *I attract ventriloquists looking for a dummy act wherever I go!*

Shiny had gotten hold of a class list. Since each overachiever had introduced his- or herself, Shiny Sheena used her crack investigative skills to uncover my true identity. I felt a bit like Wonder Woman caught wearing only her hot, red boots.

Dr. Sam gave another little nod, but I got the feeling he wasn't as pleased with ol' Shiny as she'd have liked.

"Kayla Dean," I said, standing. The auditorium seat snapped shut and rattled. Lights overhead buzzed.

"Well, Miss Dean, we are pleased to have you among our distinguished class. Tell me, do you have a specific interest or story that you're working on right now?"

What choice did I have?

With a huge sigh, I looked right at him and said, "No."

Seventeen mouths made little O's as they gazed in horror at *The Freak with No Ideas* . . . *The Monster Without a Clue* . . . *The Nellie Bly Project: How to Investigate Nothing!*

I braced myself. Would I get booed?

Dr. Sam, with his hands draped casually in the pockets of his khakis, moved quietly up the carpeted aisle until he was parallel with my row. Every neck and eyeball twisted to follow him. He was the messiah. He was the light.

For us journalism geeks, he was The Man.

He lowered himself onto the wooden arm of the auditorium seat at the end of my row.

"Well, not having an idea now is perfectly fine," he said.

Note to Shiny Hair—Perfectly Fine. Did you get that? Hmm? Hmm?

"It's not that I haven't been thinking about it because I have but I'm interested in a lot of things and I just haven't decided . . . um, figured out, which one I should focus on." I was blabbering. Couldn't stop. Wanted to, but couldn't. Then I tucked my lips inside my mouth.

"It's good to keep an open mind. Although sophomores seldom get bylines in the first semester, we encourage you all to work on projects over the summer. We always save space on what we call the second Page One, which is the back page. But if you don't make it, it's not the end of the world."

Dr. Sam stood, gave the seat back two quick taps and looked

over at me again, hard this time. "It doesn't cost anything to try, Miss Dean. The story the staff picks could be yours."

He started down the aisle and I flopped back against my upturned auditorium seat. But before he got to the bottom, he turned back toward me.

"Miss Dean?"

I sprang up like some crazed jack-in-the-box. "Yes, Dr. Sam?"

"You were just picked for the dance team, right? My grand-daughter, Nena, is on the squad. The Lady Lions?"

Once again all eyes were on me. But their pitying gasps were replaced with bug-eyed "Duh! What? Not her!" expressions.

"Yes, Dr. Sam. I . . . um, I'm a . . . on the team."

"Good, good, then. You'll have no trouble coming up with material to write about, I'm sure. My granddaughter is the light of my life and she always has something fascinating to say about that dance team. The success of that team after only five years in existence shows that students can be scholars, but they don't have to be one-dimensional."

Shiny Girl looked like she'd just swallowed a frog. The deep-down evil Kayla wondered if the frog was homeless, and if so, if it had been discriminated against. "I play the flute!" she yelled.

"Um, I coach hockey," another overachiever chimed.

Then it went on like that until Dr. Sam couldn't take it anymore. Poor man. Probably feared if they didn't quit kissing his butt soon he'd wind up going home with no skin at all. He waved them off. I was still mute, unable to think of a single thing to say.

Once Dr. Sam guided us back toward why we were there, to talk about the J-program, everybody settled down.

I slid down in my seat.

Nena is his granddaughter.

I didn't feel like a steely undercover reporter. I felt like a deceitful little deceit monger. The yellowest of yellow journalists scrounging for story bits.

How was I possibly going to write an exposé saying that his precious granddaughter was, as Rosalie claimed, part of an evil hierarchy that robs women of their natural power and leaves serious women strewn like roadkill across the cultural highway?

I was so dead.

TO: ladygodiva@bellnet.net
FROM: dragonslayer@webtv.net

Pappy doing better; we'll be back next Friday evening. Can't wait for Saturday's session. After the success of "Crown," we'll take over RPA and the Lady Lions will be nothing. "Justice of right is always to take precedence over might."—Barbara Jordan

FOR WHOM THE BELL TOLLS

Tick, tock... Kayla gets a visit from her hormonal clock. Is there cause for alarm or will she snooze and lose?

🕐 🕐 🕐 WORLD CLOCK 🕐 🕐 🕐

New York/Fort Lauderdale	8:00 **PM**
London	12:00 **midnight**
Tokyo	8:00 **AM Friday**
Paris	1:00 **AM**
Baghdad	3:00 **AM**
PUBERTY	**Thursday, 7:44 PM**

Okay, here's the deal:

What happened next on my journey into high school popularity destruction should go down in some sort of book, the annals of high school crushes skidding horribly into the fires of damnation.

Despite my open-faced drooling recently over the Gardner of the Gods, my one and only true love fantasy boyfriend was Roger Lee Brown.

Period.

Case closed.

So when my dad offered to jog with me in a nearby park—one thing Father and I had in common was that we liked to run off our frustrations—how could I know it would turn into both the high and low points of my nonexistent romantic life?

Father had barely broken a sweat when we finished our first mile. We'd run almost side-by-side. We didn't really talk, which I appreciated. That kind of bold-faced bonding would have been way too much for me. After mile two, he looked over his shoulder, winked, and sped up. By mile four, he lapped me because I was walking and wiping my forehead with the tip of my t-shirt.

"Hey, be careful. I almost could see your . . . you know," said my father. Then he sped off, looking embarrassed. My "you know" was my sports bra. Could he be more of a caveman?

By the time I peeled off toward the edge of the track, I could hear my father's feet going *boom, boom, boom* against metal bleachers. He was going up and down, up and down, making quite a clatter. I wondered what was on his mind. Like me, he took off in his gym shoes when he had to work some things out.

I definitely needed to work some things out.

My head buzzed with voices. Rosalie's voice and what she wanted. JoJo and what I thought she wanted. Miss Lavender and her comments about my look and what she wanted. Even my Mom's voice. I could hear them all buzzing in my head, telling me what was best for me, telling me how to be *Kayla*.

But the one voice I couldn't hear clearly was my own.

Sweat dripped down my neck. A thin magenta stripe of setting sunlight swooshed against the sky. My father's silhouette looked navy blue in the distance. He took off toward the trail. I was near the parking lot, stretching and sweating.

That was when I saw the car.

When it parked, I froze and when I heard the driver's door open, my breathing caught. Familiar voice.

"It's me, um, we sort of bumped into each other at the practice field. You were trying out for the Lady Lions."

Roger Lee Brown stood with his thumbs hooked into the rear belt loops of his too-big khakis. His back was to the west, which meant the darkening orange and purple sky outlined his chocolate brown body to perfection.

WARNING! WARNING! THIS IS NOT A DRILL, PEOPLE—*Roger Lee Brown is in the neighborhood park at sunset wearing khakis and no shirt.*

And talking to me!

My heart and knees did weird noodle imitations. I couldn't stop myself, I glanced at my watch:

7:44 PM—the precise moment that puberty kicked in. I felt it actually kick. I will not tell you where.

He stared.

I stared.

I frowned. "What?" I said.

He nodded toward my head. "Your hair, man."

My eyes widened. He instantly shook his head. "No, um, I mean, it's just, so . . . bushy. I mean, it's kinda dope, you know, how there's so much of it. It's all right." But he didn't say "all right"—he pronounced it the cool way—ah-ayt.

Shame! Hot, liquid shame, shame, shame!

Frogs croaked. Crickets chirped. Night birds sang night bird songs.

He said: "Hey, listen." He leaned forward against the car door as he spoke.

He was shifting from one foot to the other.

Did I make him nervous? Then an awful, terrifying thought occurred—maybe he was afraid that since I'd seen his you-know-what, I was making some kind of judgment.

Oh, great! Maybe he thought I'd seen lots. Of penises. And thought I was some sort of penis expert.

Dr. Kayla Dean,
World's Foremost Penis Peeper

I could never say "*ugh*" enough.

"I didn't really see it that good." Before I knew what was happening, it just popped out of my mouth.

First he frowned.

Then his mouth fell open and slowly he began to back away. I prayed for a dimple, a crease in the time-space continuum big enough to swallow me up. Once again I needed that runaway gator to eat me whole and save me from my nasty self.

By this point, he was moving back around the car no doubt to use it as a shield, protecting himself from Broward County's foremost penis expert and neighborhood perv. "Well, ma, I gotta bounce. Maybe one day after you get out of practice and I finish with football, we can, you know, hook up or whatever? Hang out."

He was love-song beautiful.

I was falling through space and time. He was not seeing me at my brainy best. I was a thinker. A serious young woman. I wanted to scream: **"I AM AN INTELLECTUAL, FOR GOD'S SAKE!"**

Roger Lee Brown was almost back in his car when he paused. He drummed the roof of the car. He had long fingers. He came back around the car toward me.

Was I downwind? Oh, geez. After jogging and stretching out here for nearly an hour in the heat, I smelled like bad canal water. Involuntarily, I sniffed at my pits. I didn't jab my fingers under there and take them out and sniff them, but I did sort of lower my head and take a whiff. Then I winced because it was not good.

He looked at me like I was on loan from a museum.

"Pretty bad, huh?" he said.

My mouth hung open. Crickets chirped. Frogs croaked. Cars on the road beyond us whizzed along. Night birds kept doing their thing and all that.

I said nothing.

"Um, anyway . . . yeah. So, anyway . . ." Our eyes met. The purple and orange light in the sky had vanished behind the trees. Darkness was getting thicker. He looked confident and unsure at the same time. Our eyes locked, and for a crazy moment, I thought he might actually want to kiss me.

Then . . .

"Teeeeeeeeen-hut!" my father's voice barked. "'Bout time to roll out, Captain Smarty Pants. Getting dark. Perfect time for gators to come hunting."

Then he shot Roger Lee Brown a look and said, "Son, do me a favor and step away from the teenage daughter."

I could actually hear the blood vessel in my head exploding as my head whipped around. Between clenched teeth, I gritted, **"FATHER!"**

And you know what the big ape did?

He grinned. Big, white, toothy grin.

Roger Lee cleared his throat. He was definitely trying to get away from me now. He was in his car when he called, "See you, Kayla!" Shrapnel from the tires filled the thick night air around us as he peeled away.

"You will do anything to make my life miserable, won't you?" I hissed.

At first, he looked at me with a face full of shiny defiance. Then he seemed to deflate. He let out a big exhale and started up the truck. He said, "You like him? That boy?"

Now it was time for my expression of defiance to change to one of red-faced embarrassment.

"None of your business," I said. I was not going to discuss this with him. He paused a beat, then seemed to yank the truck onto the road.

"You know, all of us are just trying to be a family. Me, ya mama, my mama, we just want to be part of your life. We can't be JoJo, but how long do you plan to keep pushing us away?"

I turned my head. It was like he'd slapped me. Was that why he'd needed to run to clear his head? Was *I* the big problem he was trying to figure out?

Blurry stars sharpened against the deepening darkness. We rode in silence for a few seconds and a whispery "yes" spilled out of me and blended in with the whirring A/C. As in, "Yes, I do like that boy." As in, "Yes, I do want to be part of our family." As in, "Yes, I do want a connection."

But my father didn't hear me. He had his army face on, eyes locked straight ahead. Hands at ten and two o'clock on the steering wheel. Jaw clenched tight.

We drove home in silence.

Even as I tried to sleep later, as I wanted to think about the sexy, chocolate, love-song heat coming off Roger Lee Brown, it was my father's voice I kept hearing. Another buzz ringing in my head, telling me I was doing a lousy job of being me.

POET EMILY DICKINSON
LIVED AS RECLUSE AND INTELLECTUAL;
DIED IN SECLUSION

Kayla makes great discovery—seclusion is for dead poets not young dancers!

Love—is anterior to life—
Posterior—to death—
Initial of creation, and
The exponent of breath.
    —*Emily Dickinson*

Degradation-elation!

Dis-bliss!

Jubil-infamy!

No one word, not even a Kaylaism, defines how I felt or what happened over the weekend.

I had never felt so—alive.

I had never wished so hard for death.

Like most calamities, it started when D-squared arrived back from her cruise. Demolition Diva gave out orders like souvenirs. She gave me a bottle of perfume and ordered, "Dear, wear this tomorrow at dinner, all right?"

Of course, my head tilted to one side and I made a Scooby-Doo-like sound, "Ruh, roh?"

She beamed brightly. "Oh, dear, you remember. My church sister, Irene. Her grandson. So adorable. Baggy pants but he comes from a good home." Then she frowned and she made the Scooby-Doo face as she looked at my hair.

"Grandmother. . . ."

Her finely arched brow rose, no doubt, because I was giving her The Tone.

"Grandma Belle," I said. We were in the living room, the whole family. The others were looking at me and I didn't know what to say. "I . . . I'm not really interested in meeting anybody."

Desperate I swung around. Amira, always looking so smug. I remembered her with my cell phone, reading my text message. I smiled sweetly. "Why don't you take Amira, Grandma Belle. I'm sure she'd love to meet Sister Irene's nice grandson."

My smile was positively beatific. (*Beatific* is a wonderful word and you can't believe how difficult it is to work it into regular conversation.)

Amira locked eyes with me. I expected her face to flush with the agony of defeat, but instead, she seemed to glow. She stepped forward like the last, insipid contestant remaining on one of those mind-numbing reality shows where Prince Charming is choosing between two poor, pathetic girls who are neither serious nor intellectual.

Her smile was as bright and fake as mine. "I can't go with Grammy Belle tomorrow because I have a date."

Aaaaaaaaaa daaaaaaaaate.

My younger, shapelier, better-traveled sister was now going to go on a date.

Before me.

I wasn't supposed to care. Didn't think I'd care.

But I cared. I cared. When God sent out breasts and curves to some girls, did he include some sort of tracking device guaranteed to *beep-beep-beep* when boyfriend-bait was approaching?

Twin daggers of humiliation and sadness sliced me. I staggered like a backup Juliet in a really bad Shakespearean production. "With who?" I asked.

"*Whom,* my dear. With whom," Demolition Diva corrected.

After that, I couldn't go on. The date was bad enough, but the grammar—well, that was too much. Simply too much.

To my retreating back and hasty goodbye, D-squared called, "Dear, please be sure to wear your pearls tomorrow, won't you." Then, in a generalized stage whisper, "If she won't do something with that bush on her head, at least we can distract the boy's eye with classic jewelry."

Ugh!

Of course, to further boost my self-esteem, I received a Rosalie update. She had taken to just e-mailing quotes. What was waiting for me before the big dinner:

TO: ladygodiva@bellnet.net
FROM: dragonslayer@webtv.net

I feel very strongly that change is good because it stirs up the system. — Texas politician Ann Richards

117

Well, I had no idea how stirred up my system was about to get.

Turns out, Miss Irene, D-squared's church sister, was the grandmother of someone I knew. Just seeing him, that was bliss.

"Kayla? Kayla Dean?" Roger Lee Brown looked as shocked to see me as I did to see him. The scheming grandmothers exchanged glances that had to be the white-glove version of high fives, signaling they'd made a good match.

Dinner passed in a blur of stolen glances between me and Roger Lee. Demolition Diva looked proud despite the near coronary she'd had when I showed up to go wearing her beautiful pearls with a "Feed the World" t-shirt and a pair of black jeans.

When it comes to how long I tried getting ready, I can't even go there. I mean, I wear mostly second-hand clothes because, it's true, I do think we as women are encouraged to bow down or whatever to a totally superficial fashion god all for the sake of consumerism.

But there's another reason.

Dressing up and getting all girly, it makes me feel stupid. I mean, it just doesn't feel like me. At least, it didn't used to. Sitting at the table with Roger, though, I wished I had some of Amira's outfits, not to mention her curves.

After dinner, the grandmothers encouraged us to walk off the sweet potato pie. Miss Irene's house sat on a canal.

"You've heard about the alligator that's supposed to be hiding in the neighborhood somewhere, right?" he said.

My heart was moving too fast in my chest and my mind had

all but stopped. I felt so out of place. I couldn't talk, so I just nodded.

We walked some more, and after a minute or so I felt I could speak without croaking like a frog. We were passing the rear side of Miss Irene's house, beside the canal. A boat bobbed gently in the slip. "Is that your grandmother's boat?" I asked.

"Pappy's," Roger Lee said. "My grandfather."

Then we walked in silence for about five minutes, until he nudged me, sort of gave me a shove with his arm.

When I looked at him, he shot me a sly grin that made my toes hot. "Shorty, your hair is mad crazy."

I was glad it was getting dark. He couldn't see the red in my cheeks.

"I remember back in the day, in grade school, your hair was all shaggy and long," he said.

"You remember me?" It just came out.

Silence . . . walk, walk, walk . . . more silence . . . birds singing . . . and then . . .

"You know I liked you, right? You were so quiet all the time. But that hair. I just wanted to pull it. Something to get your attention." He shrugged. Then he stopped and gave me a long slow smile. "But you acted like I wasn't even there. Like you couldn't see me."

Zing!

I was so flustered, I reached up and caressed the pearls, mouth open, praying something witty or provocative would please, please, please come out.

Miss Irene's property was circular and so we'd kinda circled around. I could see their screened-in Florida room in the distance pressed between several tall trees. The scent of mangoes and ripening oranges hung in the night air.

My mind whirled. I kicked around aimlessly and when I stepped up on a rock half the size of a watermelon, I turned and found myself face-to-face.

With Roger Lee Brown.

Yes, I could see him. I'd always seen him. Oh, snap! Was that a love song playing in my head?

In the dark with sweet-smelling fruit trees and a canal in the background, Roger Lee Brown looked down at my feet. "Nice kicks," he said, looking at my shoes. I blushed in the darkness. Old-fashioned Chuck Taylors. Purple high tops. Two pairs of laces — pink and white. I loved those shoes.

"Thanks," I whispered, almost unable to breathe.

He pulled me to him. Even though I was standing on the rock, he was still taller. His first kiss landed on my bottom lip. Next thing I knew, my mouth was open, his mouth was open . . . *oh, my goodness!*

Remember when I said discovering that Roger Lee Brown was Miss Irene's grandson had been pure bliss? Well, get ready to add a heaping helping of disgrace.

Right on cue, Demolition Diva's voice cut through the night and broke our spell. "Kayla! Dear! We should be going!"

Hearing her caused me to jump, which caused me to slip, which caused me to slide, which caused Roger Lee to tighten his grip around me. I'd never been that close to a boy before, know what I mean? Okay, if you don't, here's a clue:

I felt, like, every contour. And he had lots of contours. In lots of places. And me being me — **INSANE** — I didn't pause or think. Something rather hard jabbed me. So I said, "Ow! What do you have in your pocket?"

Hmm . . . I'd just been totally making out with a boy who suddenly had something hard in his pocket. Can you guess what it was? Too bad I couldn't before I opened my big, fat mouth! Oh, yeah. This was definitely the point where bliss got run over by the dump truck of disgrace.

Dis-bliss!

For a few seconds, we could only hear each other's breathing. Then he released me and stepped back like I was radioactive.

I tried to swallow — couldn't. Mouth was totally, completely, absolutely dry. My eyes watered. He was looking at me, maybe he was going to say something, but I had to get away from him.

How many penis faux pas could a girl get with one guy?

"Kayla?" The Diva's cultured voice rose above the chorus of croaking frogs.

I opened my mouth to say goodbye or something like that, but all that came out was, "Oh, my god! I . . . I . . . oh . . ."

My jubilation tonight will live in infamy.

Jubil-infamy!

ALERT THE MEDIA

Word is out. Will Kayla kiss and tell?

How many cares one loses when one decides not to be something but to be someone. — Coco Chanel

𝓙 awoke to find Amira sitting at the foot of my bed. Staring. Before I could jump out of my skin, she said, "So is it true?"

Sleep crust flaked into my eyes. "Huh?"

"You and Roger Lee Brown. You made out last night. Is it true?"

Well, no need for a double-shot latté now. My degradation-elation from the night before started as a dull tingle behind my eyes. Then it jumped into road-racing rabbit thumping in my chest.

I got tangled in my sheet, then . . .

BAM!

Hit the floor. Got wedged between my nightstand and the

bed. When I finally flipped my way out of the tangle, Amira was still sitting at the foot of my bed. Hands neatly folded across her lap. My room was still shadowy. The blinds were still closed. I could see she was wearing pink. And eyeliner.

Eyeliner. First thing in the morning. In summer. What? Was she heading out to play the love interest in Bow Wow's next music video? Her world, Planet Girl, was such a mystery to me.

"So it's true," she said.

"How did you . . . I mean . . . we didn't . . . make out. We . . . we . . ." I was on my feet, waving my arms like a crazy windmill.

Amira stood, a smile breaking across her face.

"He kissed you?"

I nodded.

"You kissed him back?"

I nodded again.

She started toward the door, stopped, and looked back at me. "Then you made out. Maybe you aren't such a total freak after all."

She gently shut the door and I raced into my bathroom, stripped off my U Miami t-shirt, and jumped into the shower. How did Amira know? My heart was beating way too fast for so early in the morning. And what was I going to say to Roger Lee Brown to make up for being such a freak show? I heard someone rap on the bathroom door. Amira. Again.

"Mrs. Roger Lee Brown," she sang out. "Your friends are here."

I yanked the curtain back. No way was I prepared to deal

JULY 18

with Rosalie. "Um, I know you and I haven't done a whole lot of that sister thing, but please, please, please make up something. Just get Rosalie to go away." What if the same grapevine that revealed my make-out secret to Amira had been accessed by Rosalie? Had the frogs outside Miss Irene's house been equipped with Webcams?

"It's not her," Amira said. "A few girls from your dance team. We're in the kitchen when you get dressed."

And once again, like a pink poof of fairy dust, she evaporated.

Okay, here's the thing: I was not ready for what was waiting for me. If I hadn't gotten up 'til noon, I still would not have been ready. Nena and Tangie grinned up at me with anxious, eager looks on their faces. And there was Mom. With the tea set.

Clink. Rattle. Jangle!

The sound of the teacups against their little saucers reminded me of skeletons jangling in the dark. The only reason she even bought the stupid tea set was because she found out once from JoJo how much I liked going to the Morikami Museum and having tea and taking part in their little tea ceremonies. It used to feel ancient and magical to me.

Now whenever I saw the tea set, I knew something was up. And the sound of the silverware and the China set my teeth on edge.

"Dear, please come down and join us. We've been waiting

on you," said Demolition Diva. She wore a neat-fitting navy blue jogging suit with white side racing stripes. "Oh, that hair!"

"What—"

D-squared cut me off. "Dear, we've been talking." She grabbed my hands in hers. "You are so beautiful, Kayla. So much promise. But, oh, that hair. Your clothes . . ."

". . . We thought maybe you were ready for a change," Mom said, cutting off the Diva.

I knew I was in trouble when I realized someone had brought out the bamboo placemats and wooden dishware. Earthy. Wild. Jungle. Whenever Mom feels she needs to make an impact, she goes all native on us and themes the kitchen. Nena and Tangie exchanged nervous glances, hands pressed flat against blond bamboo. Two ancient cultures represented at the table with the African place settings and delicate English tea set. I glared from Mom to the Diva, then snatched my hands away.

"What is this? A fashion intervention? Like I'm some sort of addict or have some sort of –ism?"

"Kayyyy-la!" Amira sang my name, stretching the syllables in grating and unnatural ways. "Look. I mean, okay, so I call you a freak and I don't understand why all your other friends take so much delight in looking and talking like costars in black-and-white movies. But you're going to a new school now. And you're going to be one of them." She pointed at Nena and Tangie. They looked embarrassed. Tried to smile.

I tried to disappear.

Amira went on. "You're a Lady Lion, Kayla. Hello? Popular. No one is going to be feeling you in that . . . that . . ."

Her finger pointed at my denim overall shorts, the ones I always wore on the weekend. "But they're my favorite," I said.

She shook her head. "Not feeling it, K. And now that you've gone and made out with the hottest, cutest guy on the football team, you can't be running around looking like some finalist for *What Not to Wear*. People will want to look up to you."

Tangie and Nena tried to jump in and save me. Nena said, "Well, me and Tangie were going to go shopping today and we remembered what Miss Lavender said about maybe hyping your look a little."

"So," Tangie went on. "Since we didn't have practice today, we thought, hey, why not go hang out with Kayla. We called last night and asked if you'd like to go." Tangie's voice trailed off.

"Kayla," Mom's voice was gentle. "We're all just trying to help."

"By ambushing me in my own kitchen? By telling me that regardless of my IQ, regardless of overcoming my shyness to achieve something so . . . so . . . amazing, that's not enough? Being philanthropic, wanting to give back isn't enough? No. It's never enough. I'm never enough. Now I've got to be some big, sexy, fashion vixen, too!"

"Kayla!" Mom said.

I was already backing away.

"Now, dear, there's no need to get so emotional. But you got on so well with Irene's grandson. He is a hottie isn't he?"

We all got wide-eyed when D-squared used the word *hottie,* and Amira said, "Grammy!"

D-squared moved around the center island toward me.

"Oh, dear. That bush of hair. You could be such a beauty. Listen to your grandmother. . . ."

"My grandmother is **DEAD!**"

Well, that got everybody's attention.

Cue the exit. I was outta there, running to hide in my room.

J know **what you're probably thinking:** That didn't go so good. Right? Well, things didn't stay that way for long.

Nena and Tangie came up to my room while I was going nuts, yanking all of my clothes out of the closet and the dresser, making a big heap. When they tried to talk to me, I started blabbering and crying. A hysterical mess, that's what I was.

But for whatever reason, I cracked. Broke down and told them everything—how conflicted I'd been feeling. How much I'd wanted to experiment with a new look, but at the same time I was afraid of changing too much or trying to be somebody I wasn't.

I also told them how I felt about spending a lot of money on clothes when children all over South Florida couldn't even afford books or shoes for school. I mean, really, that stuff's important to me.

Well, it turns out, Tangie is a very eco-friendly kind of girl. She wants to design clothes made from totally recycled products and things that are safe for the environment. Nena, a vegetarian, gets insane when it comes to companies that test makeup on animals.

"You know, Kayla, we just wanted to kinda polish you on the outside, not change you on the inside." Which led me to pull out my book of Kaylaisms and add a new entry:

Phi Slamma Glamma.

If the little coven that converged on me today were a Greek sorority, no other name would fit.

Tangie offered to braid my hair. She told me that her and Nena had found out about me and Roger Lee when they got to my house this morning.

D-squared strikes again!

Although I still haven't figured out how she saw us. Anyway, the girls spent hours with me braiding, twisting, plucking my eyebrows, applying hypoallergenic and eco-friendly products to my hair and skin.

Finally, Tangie said, "Take a look."

On the wall beside the bookshelf JoJo had left to me, the one filled with her favorite books, hung a mirror. I stared for a moment.

The smile started in my heart and worked its way out. It was like my whole body, my whole life was smiling at me. Like I knew I was being seen and I liked what people were seeing.

Feeling that way made me feel — strong.

Powerful!

I was so happy, and the first thing I wanted to do was call Rosalie. I'd have told her that looking like that made me feel like I might be taken more seriously, not less.

Then I thought about it and my face fell instantly.

"What's the matter? You don't like it?" Tangie asked.

I took a hard swallow trying not to bawl. "It's just . . . I . . . I just don't know what to say."

They smiled and Nena said, "Group hug!"

And we did.

The girls later taught me the difference between vintage chic and thrift-store crappy. After my earlier outburst, we all feared the mall would send me over the edge. We hit a few consignment shops, a few hoity-toity secondhand stores where Tangie actually shops a lot herself. Places I'd never been.

I'd spent a good bit of my savings, but I wasn't as sad about it as I'd thought I would be.

And shoes. I had new shoes. Four pairs. A pair of strappy sandals, a pair of wood-sole mules, a pair of pumps, and a pair of loafers. I am a little ashamed of how much I want to scoop them up to my chest and hug them like long-lost loved ones.

"Dear, your hair!" the Diva exclaimed when she saw me, looking like she might tear up. I got a bit misty myself. I felt really bad about what I'd said earlier. Mom was in bed so I hadn't seen her since my morning meltdown. I owed them both an apology, I just didn't know how to say it.

"Your hair is gorgeous!" D-squared said. Tangie had made cornrows going back, then left the ends loose, pulled together into a ponytail that she'd trimmed, snipped and spritzed to within an inch of its life. It did look good.

"And your clothes." I was wearing an oxford shirt and white linen khaki capris. "I . . . the pearls are great. Thank you so much." I reached out and my grandmother pulled me close.

"From freak to teenager. You need your own reality show," said Amira. Then she hoisted herself off the kitchen counter with an exaggerated yawn. "Well, toodles. I really need some sleepy-poo!"

Sleepy-poo! Who talks like that? I mean really, who?

Soon after, I was twisting and turning in my own bed wondering if I should feel, I don't know, scared, or maybe horrified—whatever—to know that my looks had the power to make me feel more powerful. Two months ago, I thought nothing would make me stronger than turning fifteen, buying a first-edition like me and JoJo talked about, and discovering my destiny.

But looking at myself in that mirror, seeing me like that, I felt—whole. What is that about?

I mean, was I that kind of woman?

Well, until I was sure, I was making sure that the scarf tied around my poofy ponytail stayed in place. Just in case I was that kind of woman, I wanted my hair to be on point.

PART 1 (PRELUDE TO A DIS)

I was capping off one of the most amazing weeks of my life—and one of the most nerve-racking.

On Tuesday, D-squared climbed back into her larger-than-life, fully repaired Lincoln and headed back to Atlanta. I have to admit, I was sad to see her go. Well, maybe not *sad*-sad, but I was going to miss her. There. I said it.

"Kayla," she whispered in my ear. "You look splendid. The hair. *Oh!* You are making an old woman very happy." Then she pulled me closer. "Not me, of course. I mean, of course I am quite proud of you and happy, but I'm not an old lady. I was referring to your great-grandmother, Hattie." Then she pulled out a digital camera, snapped three pictures with the flash aimed right at my eye, and drove off as I blinked away spots for several minutes.

At practices all week long, all of the squad, Miss Lavender and Roman included, made a big deal about my makeover. It was embarrassing and wonderful at the same time. I felt special and important and . . . great!

Then there was Roger Lee Brown. When he saw me, man! His mouth just dropped open.

"So you're all that now, huh?" he'd asked, grinning. I wanted to think my behavior at his house had been forgotten.

We talked on the phone almost every night. How do I describe that? None of the conversations were very long. He worked at his father's auto shop when he wasn't at practice, and I had been swamped with last minute SPEAK business as well as practices that were going longer and longer. We were both toasted by evening. We usually talked just before bedtime.

But every time I hung up and put my phone back in its charger, I'd find myself smiling in a way I never had before. It was a nice way to fall asleep.

Everything had gone perfect.

Then Thursday morning came.

E-mail:

TO: ladygodiva@bellnet.net
FROM: dragonslayer@webtv.net

Meeting for Saturday had been changed to 1 p.m. at the rec center on Fig Tree Lane. Lot of folks coming. Need more space than "headquarters."

Women ought to have representatives, instead of being arbitrarily governed without direct share allowed them in the deliberations of government. —Mary Wollstonecraft

That meant we'd be meeting two hours earlier than I'd planned. Then came jolt No. 2:

Miss Lavender was on a tear at practice. "Young ladies, we need to be extra vigilant about how we conduct ourselves. We are being scrutinized at all times." What she was talking about was that one of our teammates had been spotted in some booty-shake dance-off in a teen dance club a few nights earlier. She'd been wearing her Lady Lions workout uniform.

"We've suspended her until further notice," Miss Lavender said. We all gasped.

Then she told us we were in danger of losing funding from the school because the administration had been "besieged" with complaints. Looked like a lot of people had heard the same rumor or some variation of the rumor that had sent Rosalie through the roof.

"But as you all know," Miss Lavender went on, "it's a lie. We didn't take money earmarked for any other club. We earned our money and earned money for the school. We worked for it. So we're going to have to work even harder this year. That's why I've scheduled a car wash for Saturday morning at the Shell station on Fig Tree Lane."

Yep. Now I was supposed to be washing cars with my fellow dancers on the same day that I was to help host the most important meeting of SPEAK's history. And it got worse.

"Ladies, please be mindful of our image. What you do represents us all. I'd like you all to think about ways we can contribute to the community. How we can elevate our image so that we're not just seen as dancers, but role models. We shouldn't have to. Nobody asks the football team to go out and prove they are good people after winning a championship. But that's how it is for women. We're always having to prove we didn't get where we got by doing something dirty. And we're usually having to prove ourselves to other women—women who should know better."

Roger Lee Brown called the night before the car wash. I asked him if he'd come.

Again, it just popped out.

He said, "Shorty, every brother I know makes it his business to come to one of the Lady Lion car washes, fa show." That's cool for, "for sure."

The car wash was from nine until noon. It was at the Shell station kitty-corner to the rec center. I was hoping, praying, bargaining with God and the entire universe that Rosalie wouldn't find out about the car wash.

And it looked like my wish was being granted. So far, she hadn't mentioned it. And she'd called me at least four times since she got back to town last night.

We'd been together last night going over last-minute SPEAK details. We needed to make sure that she and I and the other SPEAK members did a good job of convincing the women at the planning meeting that "Kick the Crown" was worthy of media and community support.

So the day went something like this:

9:02 AM

Dad pulled into the gas station parking lot. He took one look at the Lady Lions in their bikini tops, with their ultrashort shorts, then looked at me in my denim cutoffs and white knit tee. He said: "Thank god you're overdressed."

His eyes darkened as his gaze traveled back to my dance mates. I followed his gaze and was, like, *Whoa!* It was like looking at walking, breathing pinups. Dad turned to me and—you won't believe this—he reached over and pulled me into, like, the biggest bear hug EVER.

I squirmed, but he wouldn't let go, not right away, anyway. He said into the top of my head, "That's for being my conservative little intellectual. I don't think I'm ready for you to be that . . . that . . . um, well, try not to let your shirt get wet." He looked blue with embarrassment. I jumped out of the car, mumbling goodbye. I didn't know what was more embarrassing—Dad's freakish display of parental overprotection, or his naïve belief that a wet t-shirt could in any way enhance my sad boy-girl breasts.

9:33 AM

Tangie and I were dubbed "worker bees." We accepted our roles as worker bees, scrubbing, buffing, shining, and vacuuming, while others did the more glamorous job of "advertising."

Several of our bikini-top wearing Lions took turns walking

along the edge of the gas station's parking lot, holding signs: CAR WASH $5 OR DONATION.

We worked our butts off. Just between you and me, I'd never washed a car before. It wasn't the easiest thing in the world. Most people were nice, but some were mean and nasty. The ones with the grossest cars were always the ones complaining most about the five bucks. A lot of people with cars barely dirty enough to clean, however, made ten-, fifteen-, even twenty-dollar donations.

My arms started to ache from being bent over and crouched down scrubbing tires. My lower back was killing me, too. I tried to ignore the fact that it was two hundred and eighty-five degrees outside.

12:14 PM

With my butt tooted in the air and a rag in my hand, I was vigorously applying Armor All to a rear tire when from behind me I heard, "Oh, oh, oh, my good-goobly-goo!"

I spun around.

Two boys. Mr. "Good-goobly-goo" I didn't recognize. But his friend I definitely recognized: Roger Lee Brown. I became aware of every spot on my shirt that was damp, not to mention the fact that my shorts were hiked up behind, the fact that my booty had to be shaking back and forth to the rhythm of my scrubbing motion, and the fact that I was staring open-mouthed.

Good-goobly-goo stepped forward. "Baby girl! Do fries go with that shake?"

I narrowed my eyes.

Roger Lee Brown stepped between me and goobly. "Man, chill." Roger hadn't taken his eyes off of me. Maybe he was counting my teeth since I had yet to fully close my mouth.

"This is my cousin Dante." Roger Lee nodded his head toward Mr. Goobly. Goobly was what I call a *Slangaroo.* You know, the kind of guy who says everything in that Snoop Dogg, rap-style tone, and almost every other word is some sort of slang. *Slangaroos* hop from girl to girl with their jumble of mangled vowels. *Slangaroos* are harmless, just annoying.

12:16 PM

Dante took my hand and before I could snatch it away, he'd kissed it. I could only hope that the hours and hours of car-cleaning chemicals that had coated my skin fused to form a protectant, much like rain guard on the windshield. "That's my whip you working on now, knowhatamean?" *Slangaroos* also tend to run whole phrases, such as "know what I mean," together, turning them into a single word.

"Yeah," I said, frowning. Tangie looked over. She was working on the front tire. My eyes begged her to come over and help; her eyes told me, "Girl, you are on your own."

Roger Lee Brown rubbed his hands together and grinned. "So, um, what's up?"

I shrugged. My shoulders flopped up and down as though I had no muscle control.

He kept staring and tried again. "So, it's good to see you. We've been talking all week, but man, I'm so busy. I hope we can get together again—maybe without the grandmothers."

My lips started to move, but they felt numb. Some sort of rubbery-limb muscle atrophy disease took over me. When I moved, instead of slipping into a nonchalant pose, my body jerked like I was having a spasm. The fat sponge in my hand flicked forward, slamming directly into Roger Lee, catching him, uh, below the belt, oozing white, sudsy water down his leg.

Mr. Goobly had turned around just in time to witness the look of astonishment on Roger Lee's face and the look of desperate horror on mine. "Oh, *snap!*" said Goobly. "Man, you been drizzled fo' shizzle." Then he broke into a convulsive sort of laughter that caused his body to collapse inward on itself, getting lost in the folds of his oversized shorts and threatening to expose way more of his boxers than I cared to see.

12:20 PM

"The car's ready!" Tangie called, unaware of the cool display I was putting on. I was a virtual clinic of cool.

12:23 PM

Slangaroo recovered from his laughing fit, paid for his car wash, and stood back to inspect his "whip."

"Bling! Bling! And dat's on the fo'-really-real!" slanged Goobly. "Y'all hooked a brotha up!"

Roger Lee, who, once again, had moved his body in such a way that he was using a car to shield his privates from the threat that was me, said, "Did I mention that he does not go to RPA."

I smiled.

Goobly didn't care. "Yeah, yeah, yeah, I'm a playa. I don't

have time for no uptight school like that. I gots to be where the honeys is looking for some lovin'!"

Roger Lee rolled his eyes as he climbed inside the car, then he gave me the head nod.

The single head nod.

A universal symbol of cool among men and boys. It is used in greetings, to make introductions, to show displeasure, to show pleasure, to affirm, to confirm, and to dismiss.

The single head nod.

And then he was gone. Riding shotgun with Sir Goobly.

Tangie sank down beside me on a bench under a blue-and-white-striped awning and said, "Whew! Can you believe it's almost one o'clock? I'm so hungry I could eat my brush!" She tossed the scrub brush into the pail for emphasis.

"One o'clock!"

I scrambled to my feet. "I . . . I've got to go!"

Tangie looked confused. "Hey," she called to my back as I ran toward the spot where I'd tucked my backpack stashed with my change of clothes. "Aren't you going to hang out with us after we finish here?"

"Can't," I called over my shoulder.

And I took off around the rear of the Shell station and down the path to the rec center before she could ask why.

 **PART 2 (DIS IS IT!)**

I scrambled into the restroom. Changed out of my damp, sweaty t-shirt and into a fresh, clean black tee with violet lettering. I quickly dabbed on some lip gloss and checked my eyes. (Thanks to Tangie and Nena, I didn't feel nearly so lost when it came to makeup.)

Once I was finished, I left the restroom, passed through the gaming area, and went to the glass-enclosed room where we were meeting. No sooner had I exhaled than Rosalie charged up next to me and demanded to know, "Where have you been?" She didn't sound mad, but she was looking at me like she was accusing me of something.

And I was looking guilty as sin.

Inside the large conference room everything was set up.

"The place looks great," I said, changing the subject.

Just then I heard a familiar squeal and turned. "Hey, girl!" Shavonda said. We hugged. Shavonda was among several SPEAK alumnae members who'd come to the meeting. After middle school, a lot of the girls went to different schools, but they stayed in touch with e-mails or calls.

Soon as I let go of Shavonda, I felt a light tap on my arm. Jade!

"I can't believe you made it!" Our hug was a lot less emotional. Jade was not the emotional type. She was very prim. Very proper. Still, I'd always respected her.

"Are you still dancing?" I asked as I stepped back.

She nodded. "You?"

Before I could answer, two younger girls walked up.

"Didn't I just see you across the street washing cars?" She was long and lean, probably twelve, maybe thirteen. She had that bookish look that drew bullies out of the woodwork. We'd invited about eight to ten middle school girls to come and talk about the kinds of issues they'd like to address in a few weeks at the "Kick the Crown" ceremony.

"Across the street?" Rosalie said, frowning again.

With the bookish girl was a shorter, rounder girl. She was what Demolition Diva liked to call "hippy." Chocolate brown skin, curly brown afro, probably the same age as the other girl. Way, way, way too much makeup. She said, "Yeah, at the Lady Lions car wash. Are you one? Are you a Lady Lion?"

Rosalie's eyes flashed from liquid question marks to fiery exclamation points. She cut in, "We don't have time for this now."

Curly Brown and Bookish seemed unfazed by the chill set-tling over us. They pressed on. "Do you? Dance for the Lady Lions?"

Taking a deep breath, I gave them a quick nod. My eyes darted from Rosalie to Jade to the other former SPEAK girls who'd collected around the front of the room waiting to start the program.

Curly Brown's face broke into a wide grin. She looked at her friend and said, "Told you! Told you that was her!"

With a shy, soft smile, the bookish girl said, "I think that's awesome!" Rosalie hissed something under her breath and we all went inside to start the meeting.

Bon Voyage to Joie de Vivre;
Kayla Prepares for Guilt Trip

Rosalie. She shook her authentic rain stick that Dr. X said came from an African tribal chief. (Just so you know, Mom lived in Africa off and on for many years and she swears she's never heard of the tribe Dr. X claims gave her the rain stick as a gift. Granny JoJo used to say it came from the ancient Tribe of Banana Republic.)

"Can I have your attention, please? Thank you, thank you so much. We are so, so grateful to have you ladies with us to-day!" Applause.

Rosalie looked radiant. She always did when she spoke. Her wild, dark hair pulled away from her face, making her look

145

as though she'd just blown in on the bow of a ship. She wore black capri pants to match her "Kick the Crown" shirt.

Unlike that day at dance practice, here she looked in her element. She looked confident, comfortable, and at ease. You could just tell this was where she belonged. At least, until . . .

"My name is Lourdes Sanchez, I'm with 'The Kiss' station WKSS-97.1. Didn't I see you across the street with the Lady Lions?"

It was crazy. One minute, we were explaining what SPEAK stood for and how we wanted "Kick the Crown" to become this huge annual festival that unified girls in middle school and even high school, teaching that as women we need to support each other. Stuff like that.

Then they were all looking at me, nodding and smiling, saying how great it was that I was on the dance squad. Even State Representative Natalie Weiss said she'd grown up in New York and as a little girl had dreamed of being a Rockette. "I never made it, but I still see dancers as glamorous and hardworking."

Rosalie tried to rein them in. Tried to redirect. But it was like watching a small fire surge up and consume a village.

Ideas started to zing around the room.

Zing. Lourdes from the radio: "Are the Lady Lions involved?"

Zing. Dr. Benita Carlisle, middle school principal: "Can we get the group to perform for the function?"

Zing, zing, zing! Cinnamon Styles, Channel 8 News: "What a great idea. That would make a fabulous visual for a broadcast.

We could even do some promos showing the national award-winning team preparing for the event."

Zing.

Emily and I had taken lots of notes. If everything went as discussed, our event could be larger than anything we'd ever imagined. Then came time for final questions.

Question: "Kayla, how awesome is it to be on the Lady Lions?"

Rosalie appeared out of nowhere and cut in before I could respond. "Let's just keep our focus on the school year, leadership, and how we can help you manage the school year ahead. Whether or not the Lady Lions will perform at 'Kick the Crown' remains to be seen. In the meanwhile, why not stay on point. Okay?"

"Why can't we ask questions about the Lady Lions? I'm a ninth grader at Pompano High and plan to apply to Royal Palm. Even though I have above a 4.0 GPA, I like dancing. So why can't we discuss it?"

Rosalie. "Because this is not the time. Now are there any other questions?"

My whisper hissed out. "Don't you think that was a bit harsh?"

She spun and hissed back: "This is all your fault, Kayla!"

"What is?"

She grabbed the tail of my black SPEAK tee. It was so long that it covered my cutoffs. I looked like I was wearing a mini-dress. Giving it a yank, she pulled me to the door. No one could tell about the yanking and pulling because a table blocked the view.

"We'll be right back," she sang out.

We both speed-walked to a small office at the end of the hall. Rosalie practically shoved me inside, then she was, like, "zoom-zoom!" Just off the hook. She got right up in my face and was, like: "Kayla, you know how important this meeting is. We have sponsors to whom I've given my word that we're respectable and honorable and out to promote ourselves as decent women of purpose. Emulating the likes of Dr. Condoleezza Rice, remember? Now you're turning 'Kick the Crown' into some sort of dime-a-dozen media event."

My face was burning hot and I felt something balloon in my chest. She did this . . . she did that. She didn't do anything by herself. I did just as much as she did. So did Tisha and Emma and the other SPEAK girls.

My fingers curled into fists and for a second I honestly thought about slapping the silly out of her.

Instead, I wrenched away. "Rosalie, don't you dare, don't you dare lay that on me. I am a Lady Lion. I am a Lady Lion because you begged me to try out. . . ."

"I didn't beg you to do squat!"

"Then what do you call it?"

"Call it whatever you want. You're supposed to be there to prove a point. You're supposed to be writing, getting the scoop. But I haven't seen a word yet. I think it's because you've let this whole thing go to your head. I think that you've imagined yourself in your short skirt and decided maybe that's more important than being a serious woman committed to serious business. Is that it, Kayla? Is that the kind of woman you've decided to be?"

We both stood there, panting in each other's faces.

"Rosalie, it doesn't have to be a big blow-up thing. I just thought . . ."

"WHAT?" she shouted in my face. "Omigod! You did this on purpose, didn't you? Didn't you?"

"Did what, Rosalie? This was your meeting. Just like SPEAK is now 'your club.' You can't just be involved. Anything worth doing is worth taking over."

"If you screw this up because of another one of your little chicken-fit episodes, that's it! I can't keep hanging around with somebody who can't figure out from one day to the next what kind of girl she wants to be. So which is it?"

Rosalie got even closer to me, the kind of thing animals do to intimidate one another. She lifted an empty folder from the table, waved it around. She sneered, "Let's pretend this is your little exposé for the beginning of the school year. You've written your inside story. What does it say, Kayla? Huh? Do you tell the truth and shame the devil? Or do you go on pretending to be the devil?"

That did it.

No more coulda, woulda, wish-I'd-said.

Before she had time to move, I reached up and yanked the folder out of her hands.

"Rosalie Hunter! You are a bully and a fake. Since the first day I met you, you've done nothing but boss me around. . . ."

149

"I didn't boss you around. I told you what to do because you needed somebody to."

"No!" I yelled. "What I needed then is the same thing I need now. A friend, Rosalie. Not a boss. Not a conscience. Not somebody who is constantly up in my face analyzing what I say and what I do and belittling me and making me feel bad if my views are different from hers."

"Kayla, I can't believe after all we've put into this, you're backing out. How can you do this to SPEAK?"

Her shift threw me for a second. I said, "Rosalie, aren't you listening to me? I'm talking about me and you—not about SPEAK and the Lady Lions. If me and you are cool, if we're really there for each other, it shouldn't matter what clubs we're in or what activities the other one does!"

"That's where you're wrong!" Rosalie spat. "'Courage is the ladder on which all the other virtues mount,' Clare Boothe Luce."

"Oh, please, are we going to play the quote game? How about this: 'Guilt is the gift that keeps on giving,' Erma Bombeck."

She plowed on. "You know what your problem is, Kayla? Your problem is that you're weak. You're just too weak. I should have known that if you got a taste of their fake acceptance and false popularity, you might not be able to handle it. 'The conflict is one thing I've been waiting for.' Clara Barton."

"Weak! Well, Rosalie Renée Hunter, your problem is that you're a fraud. You go around preaching about women needing to look a certain way and act a certain way; need to embrace their wooliness and all that. But I know that you secretly relax your hair!"

She gasped! "Not all the time."

"And I know you and your mother secretly pluck your eyebrows. Let's face it, Rosalie, you're always ready to send somebody else out looking like a caterpillar is sleeping on her face, but all the while, you're a hair-relaxing mother plucker! And if you want to trade insults and quotes, how about what Leontyne Price had to say? 'You must learn to say no when something is not right for you.' So, Rosalie, to you and your never-ending schemes, I'm saying N-O!"

A knock on the door snapped both of us out of our rage fogs. "Kayla, Rosalie, the women are leaving. Want to come and say goodbye?" Emma asked.

Rosalie turned to me, then Emma. She said, "Let Kayla handle it. She's in charge of SPEAK now. I don't want anything to do with it — or her!"

She tried to brush past, but I grabbed her arm. My heart was thumping. "So you're going to run off again. Is that it?" Emma shut the door. Rosalie turned and glared at me, yanking her arm free.

She shook her head. "Your grandmother would be so disappointed in you."

Then she tried to push past again, but I blocked her. "What did you just say to me?" My breath was coming in short pants.

Rosalie stepped back, cocked her head to one side. "JoJo was a real woman. She understood what it meant to give up the silly and the frilly to be authentic. To be real. But look at you, Kayla. Thinking you can bring your go-go dancing friends into a group of serious women and everyone will sing a happy song. You're a joke."

"And you're a coward."

"What am I afraid of if I'm such a coward, Kayla? Huh? What am I afraid of? You're the one trying to hide behind that ridiculous makeover. Hoping you can wear eyeliner and lip gloss and maybe people will forget what a little mouse you are underneath."

I stepped closer. Close enough to feel the heat coming off her skin. "You're a coward because the only way you know how to get what you want is to kick and pick and punch and push."

Then Rosalie started shouting, rattling off quote after quote: "Take your pick: 'You can't test courage cautiously,' Annie Dillard. 'Power can be taken, but not given. The process of the taking is empowerment in itself,' Gloria Steinem. 'If women want any rights they had better take them, and say nothing about it.' Harriet Beecher Stowe. Remember when you cared about women of substance? Remember when choosing the words of women of consequence meant something about the kind of woman you wanted to be? Remember?"

"Remember this? 'A woman must look inside to find herself. When she spends too much time looking outside, hanging onto the words of others, she does not become authentic, she becomes deluded.'"

Rosalie frowned. "I've never heard that quote before. Who said that?"

"Me. Kayla Alicia Dean."

Her mouth gaped open. Then I added, "And just so you know, despite being an accomplished pianist and the most powerful woman in politics globally, your girl, Dr. Condi Rice, I read she has a thing for shoes. Nice shoes. Just like me."

And for once, before she could give me the hand or flounce her little angry behind off, stage right, I beat her to the punch. I threw my shoulder into the door and moved toward the conference room.

I didn't look back.

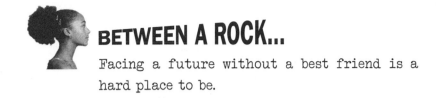

BETWEEN A ROCK...

Facing a future without a best friend is a hard place to be.

You can stand tall without standing on someone. You can be a victor without having victims. — Harriet Woods

I sat up with a start. Drums were pounding in my head. One glance at the clock told me I would be late for practice if I didn't hit the ground running.

But when I turned, I let out a scream.

Amira was sitting at the foot of my bed. *Again.*

"Amira?" I squeaked.

"Is it true?"

I let out a loud "aaaaaaaaargh!" I mean, really!

"What, Amira?" I was already climbing out of the tangle of sheets and stumbling toward the bathroom.

"You and Rosalie are on the outs? Like, for good?" She leaned against the doorjamb.

I was brushing my teeth furiously with one hand, throwing

cold water in my face with the other. "She . . ." I didn't know how to say it. What to say. How to explain it. I couldn't explain it to myself. Since that big, ugly scene on Saturday, I'd hoped some magical thing would happen and just make it all go away.

Nothing happened.

Nothing except me getting more and more overwhelmed. Almost immediately after the meeting, my cell phone started blowing up. Calls coming from everywhere. Lourdes wanting to touch base for the radio station. Then the woman from Channel 8. And so on.

Now here it was, three days later, and almost the whole world knew that in less than two weeks the Lady Lions were expected to perform at "Kick the Crown."

Except, of course, the Lady Lions. Who knew nothing because I'd been too much of a chicken to ask.

"She's just jealous," Amira was saying as I side-stepped her and grabbed a yellow jersey knit top trimmed in gray. Where were the matching shorts?

"She's not jealous," I said. Seriously, where did I put the shorts?

"Kayla, don't be a schmuck."

I found the shorts. Flopped onto the foot of my unmade bed and put them on. "Don't call me a schmuck."

"I didn't, I'm just saying, don't be so quick to act like one. She's jealous. And of course, she's terrified."

I'd dashed back to the bathroom mirror. I was attempting to spray some of the product Tangie picked out to keep a sheen in my fluffy ponytail. Amira snatched the bottle and *spritzed-spritzed-spritzed* her way around my bushy head. I turned just in time to get a snoot-full of spray.

"Amira!" I coughed and gagged.

"So why'd you turn like that?" God, please! Tell me what I've done. I'll fix it. I'll make it right. Just please, stop Amira before she gases me to death with a lethal blast of hair product.

"She's not terrified. Terrified of what?" I said. We both headed for the door, then down the stairs. Amira stayed close, but she didn't say anything until we were in the kitchen.

"You were her best minion, Kayla. Face it. Without you looking up to her, kissing her shabby butt all the time, she's just another girl in need of a moustache trim."

"Amira!" I gritted. I wanted orange juice. Orange juice and maybe one of my parents to wander in and offer me a ride to practice.

She shrugged, palms up, and was gone. And I was left thirsty and needing a bus.

Battle Fatigue:
Kayla Wrestles With a Weary Spirit

We'd begun practicing with the marching band in the mornings. Then we'd break for lunch and work out more in the afternoons. I thought gymnastics had worked me over. Now gymnastics seemed like a piece of cake next to this.

And let me just say, if practice with Roman and the other dancers had been tough, practice on the band field with the marching band, band majors, majorettes, and flag corps produced the kind of terror that could have inspired Edgar Allan Poe.

We were being berated by a five-foot, four-inch dictator, sweating beneath a four-foot tall hat, bellowing instructions through a megaphone while simultaneously bleating with a whistle as though whistle bleats were curse words.

Tommy Minors had been left in charge while Elgin, the real band major, was away at a conference. Tommy had "stand-in" fever and was giddy with power.

"... *Bleat!* You! You back there! Dancer!" He glared down the barrel of his megaphone site as though eyeing a combat target. We all froze, all of us Lady Lions. Jackie Sanders, co-captain with Rachel Glad, looked like she was about to have some sort of meltdown.

With her hands on her hips, Jackie began to charge out of formation.

Nena tried to stop her. Fear scented the humid air. It looked like the afternoon thunderstorms that came daily this time of year were going to arrive early today.

"GET BACK INTO FORMATION!" Tommy Minors the midget was screaming!

Jackie, in an explosion of speed and, I would later learn, premenstrual rage, burst up the field. She was also the anchor leg on the school's four-by-four relay team.

Large tuba players along the back line who hadn't been

paying attention and had continued to wonk out strains of "Whomp! There It Is" fell silent.

Jackie raced past brass and percussion players, past flag carriers and baton twirlers. She charged—like an angry lion—until she reached the larger-than-life stand on which Tommy Minors was perched.

"Bleat! Bleat! Bleat!" Tommy's whistle screamed, but Jackie didn't stop. She started to shake the stand.

"Somebody stop her! She is insane!" Tommy said. He looked like he'd swallowed his whistle.

"Bleat! Bleat! Bleat!" his whistle screamed again from some unseen place.

And sure enough. The stand toppled.

". . . ble . . ."

Mid-bleat, Tommy hit the ground.

My heart did a double eight-count.

Now Jackie was on top of him, and she had the megaphone, or as we had come to call it, "Tommy's weapon of mass disruption." She aimed at his face.

"LISTEN TO ME, YOU TOTAL TURD!"

Another belch of hot gusting air pushed across the field, and then we were hit with the first freckles of rain. Thin, sheer drops. The air was so hot and thick that the rain dried almost on contact.

A surge. We were moving against the exhaling winds, pushing closer to Jackie, no doubt so that we could testify at her assault trial.

Jackie kept the megaphone and yelled into it: "You are not the drum major. You are not fit to lead this band. If you try and humiliate me or my dance team one more time, I will come to your house and beat your . . ."

Woosh!

In an instant, a thick, slanting, wind-driven wall of rain replaced the near-invisible droplets. Band members scattered, clutching instruments, high-stepping for the band building. Me and Nena pulled Jackie off the tiny band dictator. Tommy Minors, in a surprising act of restraint and good sense, remained on his back, his face pointing toward the sky, unblinking.

We were breathless inside the band room. Several band members hooted and hollered. "Yo, dawg, she took him down!"

Our revolutionary zeal thanks to Jackie's initiative was short-lived. Miss Lavender came in while the band members were reenacting "the take-down." Miss Lavender had seen most of it. And she was not happy.

"Maybe we don't deserve to have a dance team," she was saying. My back ached from pressing against the concrete wall. I was wet and I couldn't catch my breath I was so dizzy with fear.

I had to tell them today. I had to tell them about SPEAK and "Kick the Crown." I had to take the chance that the Lady Lions would embrace the concept of girl empowerment.

But a squiggly worm of doubt twisted around my intestines. What if they didn't embrace it? What if they thought I was some sort of social pariah, a loser who had to make her own club just to get friends?

Would they be wrong?

". . . Reputation is the most important thing we have. Too many groups out here want to see us fail. A fight on the band field with the band major? What were you all thinking?"

"He's not the band major!" Jackie said defiantly.

Miss Lavender's eyes narrowed into black slits. I glanced at Jackie. I admired how she'd taken action earlier. Maybe tackling the viewing stand and knocking the munchkin to the ground wasn't the right thing to do. But she got her message across. She'd been fearless. "The only tired I was, was tired of giving in," Rosa Parks once said. Okay, I wasn't in a battle for civil rights, but I was tired of keeping all of my Kaylas separate. It was time for my dancing world to know there was more to me.

Before Miss Lavender could lash into Jackie again, I said, "I have an idea."

At first, no one looked in my direction. Then it was as if the spell binding Miss Lavender's intense glare to Jackie's had been broken. "What did you say?" Miss Lavender asked. The supernatural arch of her thin brows hiked to her scalp line.

Then I sucked in a mouthful of air and just let it out.

"What if the Lady Lions could show they were community-minded while being strong role models for women?" I asked.

Miss Lavender smirked and said something like, "Isn't that what I've been trying to get you guys to consider?"

So I just launched into the whole thing about SPEAK being a new club starting at RPA. I told them that our "Kick the Crown" program was two Saturdays away and stood to get a lot of advance and day-of publicity. I told her how "Kick the Crown" would be focusing on the needs and advancement of middle school girls through literacy by offering support, games, prizes, and with luck, building a sense of self-esteem.

And guess what?

She was SO for it.

They all were.

"So," I went on before I lost my nerve. "I'd been wondering, do you think we, um, the Lady Lions, could perform at 'Kick the Crown' and maybe let the TV news people come and shoot our practice to preview the event? If we got that kind of advance publicity it would be huge!"

The answer was a big, fat "Yes!" Everybody seemed so excited and genuinely enthusiastic, I wondered why I'd been so hesitant.

Of course, when Nena dropped me off at home, I knew why I'd been afraid.

Rosalie.

The squiggly worm of doubt was back. Okay, so we hadn't spoken or seen each other since Saturday. At first, I'd been like, whatever. But now, looking at the looming deadline and seeing how much had to be done, I wondered if I could pull it off?

And I wondered if I wanted to pull it off without Rosalie?

Did I really want to face a future with SPEAK if I wasn't speaking to my best friend?

Ugh!

DESTINY'S TRIAL

Independent lady must be a survivor!

You must do the thing which you think you cannot do.
— *Eleanor Roosevelt*

We were on a water break. I was hot and sweaty. And sleepy. I'd stayed up late, late, late coordinating plans for "Kick the Crown."

I took a big slurp from the fountain and let the cool water bubble over my hot mouth. I was about to dip my face under the water's arc when Tangie yelled, "K, I think your phone's ringing." I rushed over to my bag, took out my phone. A text message. It read:

U R tragic dis/pointment. Roz deserves better friend . . .

The message was from Jade.
Great. Just great.

I limped along behind my fellow dancers. Since they'd agreed to perform at "Kick the Crown," we'd been working extra. So after we finished working out on the field with the band, we took a break, then met at the gym. I smelled like livestock, honest to goodness, I really did. No amount of eyeliner or lip gloss could makeover the molten mess I'd become in the past three hours. So naturally I was overjoyed to find Roger Lee Brown leaning over the bleachers waving down to me.

He said, "Hey."

I said, "Hey."

You know, one of the things I loved about us was how well we communicated. I'd only seen him a few times this week. Too busy. He was smiling; I was staring up at him, my hand was shielding my eyes. He was a chocolaty blur.

Please, god, I prayed, let him just wave and stay up there.

He waved, then jumped over the side wall, landing a foot in front of me.

"So what's up?" he said.

I shrugged. "It's hot," I said.

He stepped closer. "Maybe that's you making it hot."

My mouth dropped open. He stepped closer.

Grass smells mixed with his warm scent. I looked up at him, then . . . my phone rang.

Text message received. It read:

U sold me out! U R a joke.

The message was from Rosalie.

Obituary notice: *The friendship is dead*

Roger Lee Brown was holding my phone. I had read the message, gasped, and taken a giant step back. He'd moved forward, then took the phone. Read the message.

"You all right? You look kinda freaked."

"I'm all right," I said. I felt shaken, like I'd been bum-rushed in an alley.

He was back in front of me, handing me back the phone. "Don't let it shake you up or nothing. I know that girl. I thought . . . you and her, friends right?"

I shook my head. It was as if the heat had found all the places where my body was tired and hung to my muscles and bones like bags of hot, wet sand. I felt exhausted. Didn't even think about kissing him.

Didn't think about too much, anyway.

He touched my cheek, then real quick drew his hand away. His touch had been cool, surprisingly cool. I looked up and he gave me this kind of weird, lame little clip on the nose with the crook of his index finger. Like it was something he'd seen in a movie.

"Don't let it mess with your head or nothing. She's just, you know, a weird, bookwormy type. Probably don't have no other friends. Probably jealous."

Weird and bookwormy. *Like me.*

By the time I got home, I'd gotten six more text messages—three from Rosalie and three from other past members of SPEAK. All angry. All condemning me.

165

At first, I'd been feeling hurt. I guess, despite the fight we'd had, I'd figured Rosalie would be working at trying to get us back together, you know, make the friendship thing tight again.

But oh, no. She had pushed the "go" button on her crazy and unleashed it like a virus.

Scientists Discover New Virus
Caused By Ego Trippin' and Too Much Spare Time—
Cure Unknown!

So when I fell into the kitchen at home, all I wanted was to get something to drink and race up to my room. I needed time to think.

Instead, I fell into the kitchen and ran smack into Mom.

She was, like, "Oh, you're home later than usual."

And I was, like, "Yeah." Didn't say "whatever," but you know I was thinking it.

I should have realized she was looking extra bright and shiny. She had on this tight white tank top and low-slung jeans. My mom has the kind of body supermodels hope to have when they grow up. But the thing about her is she acts like she could take it or leave it. She is one of the few people I know who probably exercises because she truly likes being outdoors, not because she's afraid her butt will double in size in her sleep.

Anyway, it wasn't her clothes that were all bright and shiny. It was her expression. Hopeful. Expectant.

But in my foul state of mind, I couldn't see that. Or maybe didn't want to see it. So I just blew past her to the fridge, opened it, and grabbed a half-gallon of Florida orange juice. I mumbled something about being insanely tired and hot.

The bright shininess in her eyes glowed. Still I ignored her.

Then as I tried to rush past her for the stairs, she let it drop. "Kayla, baby, since your fifteenth birthday is next Sunday . . ."

I froze. I was hot and sweaty but I broke out in a rash of "please, Mom, don't go there" bumps.

". . . Well, I know you and Mama had special plans. The book. The first edition."

I turned around slowly. I'd never discussed that with her. "How? What . . . I mean how did you know about that?"

Her dark brown eyes were liquid with need as she waved a small card at me. The postcard I'd had tacked to my bulletin board. From Books 'n' Books. Without even thinking, I snatched the card. "Why do you have this? Why were you in my room?"

"I-I just thought . . ." Mom was stammering.

Then when she took a step back, I felt myself fill up. Like, *whoosh!* A fire inside me, all the anger, pain, frustration, exhaustion, everything from the past several days that I'd buried under the surface—oh, yeah, it surfaced. I went off:

"Why can't you just let it go? You are not JoJo, all right? We can't make up for all the time we've lost. Me and you and the whole mother-daughter thing, it's not happening. Don't you get that?"

I was ranting, pacing, foaming at the mouth. Now if I was her and my daughter said something like that, I'd tell that girl she needed to get out of my house. I swear, I wouldn't take that from some mouthy teenager.

167

At least, when I pictured myself as the mother of a mouthy teenager, that's how I saw me handling it. Never really pictured myself as the mouthy teenager.

Mom, however, looked more determined. She grabbed both my shoulders, looked right at me, and said, "Kayla! The mother-daughter thing with us is working, okay? It is working? I am your mother. You are my—" Her voice broke. She took a breath.

"You are my big, beautiful, intelligent oldest child. Kayla, I love you and I want—"

"Mother!" I said it with The Tone. "I know about the biology, okay? I know you're my mother. So stop trying to force these touching moments like you're producing a long-distance commercial for Sprint."

She released her grip, took a step back. I snatched away. Have you ever been so mad you actually felt yourself vibrating from the inside out? That's how it was for me.

I was almost out of the kitchen when she said, "Kayla." Just said my name. Not loud. Not soft. Just *Kayla.* I stopped.

"What about your birthday? I was thinking we could go pick up your book, maybe plan to have dinner and cake with the rest of the family."

I turned slowly, still vibrating from the inside, hating myself for talking to her like that, hating myself for being too dumb or stubborn or dumb and stubborn to reach over and accept the love she wanted to give. Hating myself for using her as a whipping post for the anger and frustration that had been building inside of me all summer.

"Mom, I do not want to go to the bookstore with you. I do not need to go to the bookstore with you. The trip to the bookstore was going to be special because it was supposed to be me and JoJo. Me. And JoJo. Not me and you. I thought you were supposed to be trying to get back into photography, now, anyway. Now that you finished putting your life on hold for your husband."

Her eyes blazed. "Kayla! That's enough. You're not being fair. I didn't just put my photography on hold for your father. I did it after we came back from Africa because I wanted more time to be with you. To be with both my girls."

Inside my chest burned like some crazy acid was being squeezed right out of my heart. But I shook my head and said, "JoJo always said you lacked determination. She said you never took your work or yourself seriously. Well, I do. I'm really stressed right now. I've got a lot on my mind. I don't care about my stupid birthday. Just forget it, okay?"

An entire third-act drama of emotion played across my mother's face. She went still and she gave me a tight little nod.

And I went to my room where I slammed and locked my door, went into the shower, blasted the water as high and hot as I could stand it, and cried until the mirrors were fogged and the water ran cold.

THE DEAD ZONE

Trapped in an angry void, confused Kayla needs to bury her ghosts.

You never find yourself until you face the truth. — Pearl Bailey

Zombification. The act of becoming or acting like a zombie. Which is what happened to me all day long after that awful scene at home. Practice the next day was *brooo-tal!*

Couldn't concentrate. Couldn't keep up. It got so bad, even Roman wouldn't yell at me anymore. They actually kicked me out of practice. "Your mind is elsewhere, Baby Diva, so you need to be somewhere else, too." *Ouch!*

BREAKING NEWS . . .
Kayla Dean confronts the truth — and Rosalie Hunter!

So after spending the day avoiding home, avoiding my reflection in storefront windows . . . avoiding everything, I realized something.

The crappy feeling wasn't going away. And I needed to re-claim my spirit.

JoJo would have liked that. She used to tell me, never let life pull you down so far that you can't reclaim your spirit. She said I needed to always be willing to ask myself the tough ques-tions and not be afraid of the answer, no matter how my an-swers made somebody else feel.

And my "answers" were simple:

I liked being a Lady Lion.

I liked being involved with SPEAK.

I liked how I was beginning to feel about myself — except the way I'd been feeling the past few days, being such an over-the-top dragon drama queen. Komodo Kayla!

So, before the day was over, I took a deep breath, then did what needed to be done.

I went to Rosalie's house. She answered the door with a look of shock. Then a scowl.

"What?" That was her total greeting.

I didn't answer. Just pushed past and went into head-quarters.

"I'm busy, Ms. Dean. I am planning a protest at the ma-rina because some selfish yachters think their leisure time is more important than the health of the manatees. So I don't have time for—"

"Rosalie," I said. "Shut up." I said it matter-of-fact-like. Not angry or loud, just simple. Shut up. So simple, in fact, that she actually did shut up.

Her eyes were huge and round, then narrowed. She flopped

hard into a chair across from me, but I stayed on my feet, hands on hips. "Rosalie, stop sending me text messages, you hear? And stop organizing your little goon squads to send text messages. If you need to talk to me, just call me."

Nothing. She just gaped at me, then she grinned. "You're here because you know you can't do it without me. You came here to beg me to come back and take over, right?"

She sounded so hopeful. So gleeful. So filled with the need of my failure to make her feel strong again.

I shook my head slowly. "Sorry, Rosalie, no begging. I really wish you would come back. I wish you would reconsider and accept that maybe all kinds of girls have something to contribute, not just the girls you pick."

She looked like I'd punched her. Instead of jumping up and getting in my face, she sagged back in the chair. "I can't believe you'd pick them over me," she said.

I shook my head again. "No, Rosalie, I'm just picking me. Here's the thing: I know how important SPEAK was for you, but you seem to have forgotten it was important to me, too. Look, I'm not here to point fingers or play dirty. I just wanted you to know we don't have to be nasty to each other. No more texting, all right? Me and the rest of the girls are swamped getting this thing together. You want back in, just let me know."

She looked up at me, but she stayed in the chair. She said, "Being around them, it's making you crazy. You're not acting like yourself."

"Rosalie, did you ever ask yourself, of all the make-a-name-for-ourselves projects we could have done to launch SPEAK, why the first thing on our agenda was to take down the most powerful group of girls at the school?"

She looked confused. Shrugged. Said, "They aren't our type of girls." She stood, paced. I caught her arm.

"Even if that's true. Even if there's a 'right' type and a 'wrong' type and we somehow have cornered the market on right, why is it that instead of building them up to make them even stronger, we—and by 'we' I mean you—feel the need to tear them down?"

She yanked away from me, her eyes hot and shiny. She almost snarled, said, "We—and by 'we' I mean me and you—we can't go back to being friends like we were before. It can't be the same. Not with you . . . you like this!"

I shook my head. "No, Rosalie, we can't."

One truth down,
One to go

Father left for North Carolina. Something to do with the military. A couple times before he left, I'd caught him glaring in my direction. My mom had been like a ghost in the house—I knew she was there, but I hadn't seen her.

Later that night, after he was gone, I was having trouble falling asleep, so I headed down to the kitchen. Halfway down the stairs I heard a strange sound.

Voices? It was hard to tell, but it didn't seem right for that time of night. I crept back up the stairs and followed the semi-circular hallway to my parents' bedroom door.

It wasn't closed all the way. A light from the television flickered inside. My mom sat on the bed, a box beside her. She had her back to me and her face in her hands. She was crying. Softly. But deeply.

I drew a deep breath and did the only thing I could do.

Oranges on a little tree,
So sweet, so round.
Mama reaching up to me,
Am I afraid to look down?
Smaller and smaller,
That is how she looks
As I rise into the sky.
Mama will you remember me,
Now that I've learned to fly?
— *Kayla Dean, 5th grade*

Clink! Rattle! Jingle!

When I'd realized she was crying, I practically ran down to the kitchen, went in the pantry, and pulled out the little tea set from The Morikami.

"Mom," I called from the doorway. She turned around, quick, like I'd startled her. "Can I come in? I brought tea."

All of a sudden she was laughing and crying so I started laughing and crying, and she ran around the bed to get to the tray and we almost collided.

We settled ourselves and left the tea set on the bureau. I blurted "I'm sorry" over and over and started bawling harder. She pulled me to her and just held me like that for a while.

Black sky and night looked back at us. And our reflections.

We were sitting on her bed now, Mom's arm still locked around my shoulder; my head resting against her shoulder. Her holding on. Me not pulling away. Since the second floor was a circle, her bedroom had a semicircle of windows like mine. And like mine the room looked out into a dense blackness. Darkness made of nighttime sky and thick bushes.

I tried to make myself smaller, tried to shrink into her like I was going to sneak back into the safety of the womb. My voice felt smaller, too, when I said, "I miss JoJo so much. So much it hurts."

Mom turned to face me and when she did I saw tears glittering on her cheeks. "Me, too."

Then I got a chill. Like a big, freaking shocking chill that shot through me. As much as I missed JoJo, I still had a mother. Mom didn't. It was as if she sensed the change in my body language. I climbed onto my knees then pulled her head against my chest.

We switched roles. Now I was comforting her. She let her head sag against me. "I'm so sorry, Mom. I'm so sorry. I guess I was so busy feeling sorry for myself, I couldn't even think about the fact that your mother was gone. She was just my grandmother. I've been so selfish. I'm so, so, so sorry."

She pulled away, told me to let her be the mom. We both laughed, shaky little laughs that fell out between sobs. Then we started talking. Really talking. And it was absolutely great.

I told her she was right. "JoJo could be bigger than life, overwhelming sometimes. She had so many ideas. And she was never wrong, you know? Most of the time, just being with her, I was in awe of her confidence, her faith, her strength—"

"But," Mom cut in, "figuring out who you were with such a strong, outspoken person around telling you who you should be, it was tough, right?"

I nodded.

Then she told me how much she admired me, how much she believed in me. That meant a lot. "Kayla, Mama always taught me to be strong and be certain about the kind of woman I wanted to be. But what I've learned is that the best kind of woman any girl can grow up to be is one that is capable of growth, capable of change. Mama wouldn't want you to stay stuck in being who you were two years ago if that wasn't right for you today."

Dang. Really, sometimes moms are the absolute best.

THE JUMP OFF

Sophomore year is just the beginning!

Crunktacular!

Okay, work with me on this. *Crunk* is already a made-up word. Southern rappers, Miami I think, came up with it. A verb. As in, "Hey, let's get crunked." Like getting hyped, psyched, wil'ing out, like that. A *crunktacular,* then, is an event whose very nature is hyped up, psyched out, and leads to extra-wild reactions. Just so you know, these are very, very good things.

So, with only thirty minutes remaining until the close of "Kick the Crown," I had to admit it a had been a *crunktacular!*

Time for my closing speech. The Lady Lions were dancing as the finale. Yesterday we were on the radio and television. Now there were cameras everywhere. At least a hundred and fifty girls had showed up, not to mention curious teachers and some parents and librarians.

And Roger Lee Brown. He was standing to the side of the small staging area, smiling. He'd given me a soft, quick kiss on the cheek earlier. For luck.

"I just want to thank everyone for contributing to a spectacular event," I began. Over the past several days Mom and even Amira had helped, along with the other SPEAK members and their parents. We hung flyers, stuffed bookbags, wrote thank-you letters, picked up decorations, made banners—everything.

"Kick the Crown" started at noon, but I'd gotten to the park around nine. I looked out at all the young faces. Girls who'd be sixth and seventh, even eighth graders when school started. I said, "People might want you to fit into a mold, be a certain kind of girl. My advice: try being many kinds of girls. Break the mold. Be funny and a brain; cute and athletic; shy and tough. Why settle for being just one type of girl? I say be greedy and be as many types as you need to be true to *you!*"

When I'd started out, I was sort of shaking. But toward the end, I was really feeling it. Funny thing, though, was that I wasn't really looking at anything. Between the bright TV light in my face, the sun, and the sea of shining middle school faces, everything was a blur.

Then, right at the end . . .

Rosalie.

She was standing not too far from Roger Lee Brown. My heart was pounding when I finished the speech, but I was smiling, feeling good. Then I looked down right into Rosalie's face.

And here's the really funny thing:

She was kind of smiling, too. Okay, not a smile. But not a frown. Definitely not a frown or a glare. For Rosalie, that was something.

The reporter from Channel 8 took the mike and introduced the Lady Lions. We all wore black tees with lilac letters that spelled SPEAK across the chest. We also had on stretchy black jazz pants and black sneakers.

We had decided for our first public performance we wouldn't go nuts. Nice and easy. An exhibition of sorts. Music loud and fierce pumped and Roman bit his lip from the corner like a stage mother in the wings.

When we were done, I couldn't believe the rush I got from the crowd's reaction. People were high-fiving and screaming. Boys I hadn't even noticed, probably just in the park for other things, had found their way near us and were hooting and carrying on. It was crazy.

Mom grabbed me into her arms as soon as I made it off the stage. "You did good, Baby. I'm so proud," she said.

Dad, back in time to see the show, was holding the video camera. He tilted his head so the camera wasn't hiding his face. "I don't like all of that butt shaking," he said. Mom hit him. "But you did good, Captain Smarty Pants."

"Did you guys see where Rosalie went?" I asked.

Amira was standing beside Dad. "I saw her a leave just as you all were finishing," she said and shrugged.

I stared toward the exit, frozen for a moment until Tangie came and grabbed me to come and join the others.

NEW YEAR, NEW YOU

School starts in a week. I've thought about my sophomore writing project for journalism class. No exposé, but I will be writing about SPEAK and the Lady Lions. I've already started.

Tonight we were out back. Dad grilled some chicken and steaks. It was my birthday. I'd told Mom I didn't want to go to a restaurant or anything. Too tired. She was cool with that.

"Captain Smarty Pants, think you can get off your butt long enough to carry this tray?" My father smirked. I rolled my eyes at him, got up, marched over, and took the tray to the patio table. He gave a crisp salute.

Amira was out back with a friend of hers from school, not her date—he'd been a bust, by the way. We ate dinner, listened to tunes from the iPod, and I felt like something was different, but I couldn't put my finger on it.

Mom asked Amira and me to be in her second wedding on their anniversary in a few months. I was too choked up to speak. "I don't know what to say," I said.

"Just say you'll do it." She smiled.

"Just say you'll keep styling your hair," Amira added. *Ugh!* Then Mom asked about Rosalie.

"So you girls still aren't speaking?"

I shook my head. "I don't want to not be her friend, you know?" Mom nodded.

Later we had cake, and then it came time to open presents. Mom squeezed my fingers as she slid two bags out from under the table.

Both Amira and I gasped.

Shoe store bags. Two. Filled with shoe boxes. The three of us sank into the grass surrounding the patio and ripped into the boxes like we were five and it was Christmas morning. Patent leathers, soft soles, medium heels, shoes with laces, shoes with straps.

"You and mama had your thing; we'll have our special thing. I love shoes, too!" Mom said. Then the bell rang, and Mom and Amira exchanged glances.

"What?" I asked.

Mom smiled and Amira shot up and raced into the house. A few minutes later she came back.

And Rosalie was with her.

Scientists Mystified:
In Midst of Global Warming Crisis Hell Freezes Over

Rosalie came into the yard. Mom squeezed my arm. "She wanted to be here," Mom whispered.

"Hey," I said.

"Here." Rosalie jammed a package into my hand. "I, um . . . I picked it up for you. You should have it."

Inside the wrapping paper was Jane Austen's *Emma*. My first first-edition.

"But how . . ."

"You know Dr. X and Liz at Books 'n' Books go way back."

I was a little teary-eyed. I stood, reached for her, and we hugged.

She let go, then said on a breathy exhale, "Can you believe how many girls came to 'Kick the Crown'? When school starts, I'm sure SPEAK will be one of the most talked-about groups."

And just like that, I figured, well, she's back.

We cut the cake, hung out, then Rosalie had to leave. I returned to my stack of shoes, admiring them. Amira stretched her foot out, trying for a fit. Then my father appeared with his camera, shaking his head and mumbling, "Women going to drive me into the poorhouse. Shoes. Who needs all those shoes?"

"Baby, shush and take the photo," Mom said.

He gave me a pretend stern glare, fixed his camera on the tripod, and said, "Wait, I want to be in the picture, too."

And just like that, I understood the funny, different feeling I'd been having all day.

I had finally made it into the family. And the family had made it into me.

Of course, it wouldn't be a true Kayla day without one final bit of ridiculousness.

"Come on, try on a pair of the shoes, Captain Smarty Pants. Model for us!" So I took out a pair and started prancing around. Mom, Amira, everybody was whooping and carrying on, so at first I didn't hear the bushes rustling behind me. Then, just as the camera flashed, the Great Oppressor turned into the Great Protector, lunging to my rescue.

Oh, yeah. I have the picture. Right before he lunged. There I was, hands on hips. Strappy, black leather sandals showing off my legs. And the runaway alligator's snout sticking out of the bushes.

Now really, what's more ***stankalicious*** than that?

★ Lexicon of

KAYLA-ISMS

Lexicon of Kayla-isms

Astromiraculation *(as-troh-mih-rah-kyoo-lay-shun)*
An act so miraculous that it exceeds the boundaries of Earth and space.

Blind-sexy
When someone looks so good even a blind person would go, "Mmm!"

Bubblebot
Robots programmed by men to act like Stepford wives.

Crunktacular *(krunk-tah-kyoo-ler)*
An event that's very nature is hyped-up, psyched-out, and leads to extra-wild reactions.

Dare-glare
A second cousin to the evil eye, a nonverbal double dog dare.

Deflatamonium *(dee-flay-tuh-moh-nee-um)*
When you start out feeling way too good, when you dare to have hope, when your heart is all pumped up, then along comes someone who deflates you at such a rate that the very act of deflation becomes an event.

Degradation-elation *(deh-gruh-day-shun ee-lay-shun)*
When your elation turns to degradation so fast that your head feels like it will spin off.

Dis-bliss *(diss-bliss)*
The point at which bliss gets run over by the dump truck of disgrace.

Funktaciousness *(funk-tay-shuhs-ness)*
Boldness in the case of fashion or high spirit.

Funktivity *(funk-tih-vih-tee)*
Stankaliciousness run amok.

Gyroscopic wow *(jy-roh-skah-pik wow)*
Filled with color, movement, and lots of power.

Humilaration *(hyoo-mil-uh-ray-shun)*
The combination of extreme humiliation and frustration.

Joygantic *(joy-gan-tik)*
Huge with joy.

Ju-mongous *(joo-mun-gus)*
Bigger than humongous but smaller than ginormous.

Jubil-infamy *(joo-bul-in-fuh-mee)*
When your jubilation becomes so out of hand that your behavior
goes down in infamy.

Phi Slamma Glamma
If surprise makeovers were run by Greek sororities.

Rosilaw *(rose-uh-law)*
The rules according to Rosalie Renée Hunter.

Stankalicious *(stank-uh-lih-shus)*
1) Derived from *stank,* slang for *stinker,* the art of being stanky;
2) One who behaves in a manner so overboard, so bigger-than-life
outrageous, so self-deluded, that it could only be considered
stankalicious.

Slangaroo *(slang-uh-roo)*

The kind of guy who says everything in that goofy, rap-style tone, and almost every other word is some sort of slang; slangaroos hop from girl to girl with their jumble of mangled vowels; harmless but annoying.

Zombification *(zahm-bih-fih-kay-shun)*

The act of becoming or acting like a zombie.